CULLY &
THE GUNRUNNER

ORRIS SLADE

Contents

Chapter 1

A brisk wind blew over the land and the smell of rain was in the air when Cully rode toward the livery stable in Durango. Samson needed new shoes, and Cully was going to get him the best ones possible. Leaves blew across the road as Samson trotted past the Durango town limits sign.

Cully, relaxed and smiling, had just finished a week of fishing and hiking in the Colorado mountains. Spending time in forests and mountains always gave him a contentment he never found anyplace else. The scenery had been breathtaking and the pink-orange sunsets and the yellow-red sunrises had been among the most beautiful he had ever seen.

His father, a pastor, liked to quote the verse from Psalms, "I will lift up mine eyes unto the hills, from whence cometh my help. My help cometh from the Lord, which made heaven and earth." Looking at the Colorado mountains, you could easily believe the Lord would speedily come from the hills and answer an earnest prayer.

The weather had been good on his camping trip, and so had the fishing. Cully wasn't a great cook, but he had fine fish to fry, and even with his limited cooking skills, the fish had tasted halfway decent. Now that he was rested and refreshed, he wanted to get the new shoes for Samson so his horse could feel better too.

Although his usual stomping ground was Pueblo, he knew the owner of the livery stable in Durango. Actually, he knew a great many people in the Pueblo-Durango region of Colorado. As a part-time bounty hunter, he had tracked down many an outlaw in the region. Those folks he didn't know as bounty hunter, he knew due to his time served as a deputy federal marshal.

As the livery stable came into sight, he saw Ike Hodges hammering a horseshoe in front of his business. Hodges was a big man who could easily handle the hammer associated with the blacksmith trade. But Hodges probably appreciated the cool temperature and the breeze. Any blacksmith can work up sweat.

As he raised the hammer, Hodges looked up. "Cully! Howdy. What you doin' in town?" he said. Half the people in Durango now knew Cully had come to town. Hodges's normal voice was almost a shout for most people.

"Coming back to civilization from a week in the wild. Got some good hunting and fishing in. Now I need some new shoes for Samson here."

Hodge nodded. "I can do that. Just put him in one of the stalls. I can start workin' on him later today. But not sure I can finish by sundown."

Cully climbed down from Samson. "That's all right... no hurry. I'm planning to stay the night in the hotel."

"The food's good in the restaurant, too." Hodges laughed and pointed the hammer at Cully, as if to emphasize his point. "In fact, the town is coming up in the world. A month ago, we got a fine men's and women's clothing store. Townsfolk are lookin' better than ever."

Cully laughed. "Don't get too spiffy. I don't want to wear a coat and tie when I ride to town."

"Don't think we'll get that fancy."

Cully led the horse into the stable, found an empty stall, and eased Samson into it. He took his saddle off and checked to see if there was fresh water in the bucket hanging on the wall. Hodges shared his affection for horses. He kept his stalls in good condition, stocked with hay and water.

As he took the bridle off, a rider walked his sparkling, golden mount into the stable. Cully knew good horseflesh, and the stallion was breathtaking. Gold and white. One of the finest horses he had even seen. The rider was less impressive. While the horse was handsome, his rider was ugly. There was no other word for it. He was stocky and medium height, with deep-set black eyes. His crooked nose had been broken at least once. The large lips gave the man a surly smile.

Although the rider didn't look friendly, Cully walked over to the golden's stall. "Howdy," he said.

The rider said nothing.

"That's one of the finest horses I've ever seen."

"Thanks, but keep your hands off him. Stormy is mine."

Cully saw the Circle K brand on the horse. Odd, he thought. Circle K was a ranch near Silverton. It was owned by a man named Art Hadrane. He had passed through the area often and had met Hadrane. Cully didn't know the man well, but he thought it odd Hadrane would sell a horse like this golden stallion. Hadrane had three sons and daughters, and good horses were kept for his family members.

"Mister, I don't like the way you are eyein' my horse," the rider said. The man had a low, guttural voice.

"My name's Cully."

"My name is Jack Hogan. Now that we've said hello, you can say goodbye."

Cully shrugged. He didn't want any trouble. But he thought it a shame such a fine horse was owned by such a jackass of a man. He walked out of the stable, smiling at Hodges as he passed. Cully had dealt with many outlaws, and he wondered if Hogan's picture might be on a wanted poster. He started toward the hotel but paused when he passed the sheriff's office. He turned and went in.

A deputy stood by a desk and raised a coffee cup to his lips. After he swallowed, he waved. "Cully, haven't seen you for a while."

"Lately I've been catchin' fish instead of catchin' men. How've you been, Jacob?'

"Fine and dandy. What can I do for you?"

"Just wanted to browse through your posters, if you don't mind."

"Be my guest."

Cully walked over and took the posters off the wall. He skimmed through them. He saw two men who had obviously had their nose broken at some time in their life, but neither one looked like Hogan. Neither did the other men on the posters. Cully was a bit disappointed. He hung the posters back on the wall. "Thanks," he said as he walked out.

"Drop by any time, Cully."

When he walked out of the sheriff's office, he still felt a nagging itch, like a thorn was stuck in his shirt and scratching him. He would have bet a good amount of money that Mr. Hogan was wanted somewhere for something. And whatever he was charged with, he was guilty of, Cully was sure of that.

He sighed and headed across the street where he had spied the telegraph office. When he walked in, a balding, stout man was seated behind the counter, a green visor on his head.

"Yes, sir. What may I do for you?"

"I'd like to send a telegram to the sheriff in Silverton."

"Yes, sir."

The clerk grabbed a pencil. "What would you like the telegram to say?"

"Seen horse over here with Circle K brand. Gold and white stallion. Beautiful. Rider made me suspicious. Any horse stealing been reported there? And sign it Cully."

"Yes, sir. I'll get that off immediately. That'll be fifty cents."

Cully offered him a dollar. "Just make sure it gets out immediately. I'd appreciate it."

"Yes, sir. If I get a return, where can I find you?"

"Probably at the hotel."

Outside the telegraph office, Cully paused. He pulled a bag of tobacco from his shirt pocket. He found the cigarette papers, and a minute later he stuck the cigarette in his mouth and lit it. He took a deep puff.

Maybe I'm overreacting, he thought. He had no proof of a crime, just a surly, ugly cowboy. But if that were a crime, thousands of men would be in local jails all over the west.

Also, Silverton wasn't that far from Durango. About fifty miles separated the towns. *If I had stolen a horse, especially a horse that was so distinctive and memorable, I wouldn't spend a night in a town so close to where I stole it. I'd keep off the main roads and stay out of towns until I put a hundred or more miles between me and the scene of the crime.*

The thought sobered him.

He walked to the hotel and rented a room for two nights. When he came out of his room and exited the building, he glanced down the street toward the livery stable. He frowned then started the walk down the street.

Surprisingly, he heard noises as he walked up to the stable. Hodges was hammering something. He had a lantern hanging from the ceiling to give him light. He was bent over an anvil but rose up when he saw Cully. "Forget something?" he asked.

"Nope, just wanted to take another look at that stallion."

"Go ahead. Sure is stunning, isn't he?"

"He sure is." As he looked at Stormy, Cully noticed a bandage on his right front leg. "Is there somethin' wrong with him?"

"Had a bad cut, pretty deep. He was limping a bit when he rode in."

"Really. Will he be all right?"

"Oh, yes. He'll be fine. He needed some care, but after a little medication and treatment, he will be as good as new in a few days. He does need some rest. I suggested he not go out on the trail for at least two days, and three would be better. The owner argued with me and got angry, but I told him it takes time to heal."

"That was Mr. Hogan?"

"That's what he said his name was." Hodges put the hammer down and leaned against the wall. "But you know, I just got a feelin' that the so-called Mr. Hogan ain't got a reputation for honesty. So I'm guessin' he wasn't born a Hogan. We nearly got into it. He wanted to ride Stormy out tomorrow morning. Told him that was impossible. Riding him now would cripple the leg, and the horse would have to be shot. He might go for two or three hours, then the leg would go out from under him, and he wouldn't be able to walk."

"Stormy is such a valuable animal, no owner would want that to happen."

"I may have finally talked some sense into him. He said he'd wait at least two days before leaving town. He's not waiting patiently, but he's waiting.

"I figure that's why he came in. He knew the horse was goin' lame. A man without a horse in these parts is a pitiful creature."

Hodges nodded.

Cully walked to Stormy's stall and took one last look at the stallion. He was munching hay and looked content. He didn't seem to be in any pain, which he was grateful for.

He headed back to the hotel.

~****~

The next morning, he had a good breakfast at the Blue Mountain Restaurant. He was cutting into his scrambled eggs when the telegraph clerk walked in and rushed up to him.

"Mr. Cully, the hotel clerk told me you had come down here."

Cully put down his fork. "Yep, what's up?"

"Your telegram, sir. It came this morning. You gave me such a good tip, I wanted to make sure to hand it to you personally." Which he did.

Cully read it and clenched his teeth.

Circle K raided three nights ago. Several horses stolen. Among them was a gold and white stallion. Art Hadrane offering $500 reward for return of horse. $250 for capture of horse thief.

Cully nodded. Art had put a higher value on the horse than the thief. "Thank you, sir. Would you do me a favor?" he asked the telegraph clerk.

"Of course."

"Take this over to the sheriff and tell him that gold and white stallion is in the local livery stable."

"Yes, sir."

~****~

Hogan snapped the bridle on Samson. Horse thieving was a hanging offense. As much as he liked Stormy, the horse wasn't worth dying for. Last night he thought he could stay two days in Durango. But it was too risky. His fingers rubbed his neck. If he were caught, the rope would go right around there...

But to get away, he had to steal another horse. This one belonged to the dang talkative cowboy who was in the stable yesterday. Hogan lifted his boot into the stirrup and swung his leg over Samson's back. As he rode out, he saw Cully walking toward the stable. He yelled and tipped his hat.

"Thanks for the horse, cowboy!"

Cully didn't look upset at all. In fact, he was smiling. As Hogan rode by, Cully almost chucked. Then he whistled. A high, lyrical whistle.

Samson neighed loudly and reared back. He walked on two feet briefly, his front two legs raised high in the air.

Hogan yelled with alarm. His hands slipped from the reins. He tumbled over Samson's rump and fell to the ground. He rolled over and when he looked up, Cully held a pistol on him.

"Thank you, Mr. Hogan. You have made this a seven-hundred-fifty-dollar day for me." He showed a wide smile. "Samson is well trained. I guessed you noticed that. When I whistle, he comes. Oh, by the way, horse stealin' is a hanging expense. If you don't have the money for your funeral, don't worry about it. It's on me. I hate to burden the taxpayers."

Chapter 2

Running Horse shouted in triumph then pulled the cork from the whiskey bottle with his teeth and spit it out on the ground. He raised the bottle and took a huge gulp of the liquor. He shook his head and shouted again. Ten yards away, a dozen renegades, war paint on, broke open crates holding other whiskey bottles. A dozen others opened three cases on a wagon that revealed new Winchester rifles. They howled with glee.

"A piece of advice, chief. Don't drink and shoot at the same time. You'll have bad aim after drinkin' whiskey," said Mel Sandford, grinning broadly.

He stood beside his horse as he watched the men grab the bottles and guns. Sandford rarely ever smiled, but today was an exception. He was grateful he found this group of rebels. *Are they from an Apache tribe?* His wide grin showed two gaps in the upper and lower molars and tobacco stains on his teeth. He wore a two-day-old black-beard stubble.

The three outlaws who rode with him sat silently on their horses. Even though they had dealt with Running Horse's men before, they were uneasy around the renegade band. Only Sandford appeared to be having a good time.

The group's leader took another gulp of whiskey.

"OK, chief, let's get to your end of the deal," Sandford said.

Running Horse nodded and waved at his warriors. He walked to his horse, grabbed a packet, and tossed something to Sandford. The outlaw opened it. He reached in and brought out a wad of cash.

"You promised to pay for the fire water and rifles, and you sure did. Thank you, chief. And the rest?"

Four men escorted a dozen horses toward the three outlaws.

"They were stolen in what you white men call the Arizona Territory," Running Horse said. "Fine horses. All of them."

Sandford nodded. Since they were stolen in Arizona, it was doubtful anyone in Colorado had heard of the theft. So no one would ask questions when Sandford and his gang sold them. He glanced at the horses, and all of them looked prime. Two stallions, a solid black and a brown and white. Both looked as if they could race forever. At least eight geldings—the preferred horses of Westerners—that were first rate.

Dealing with the Apaches and stealing horses were both hanging offenses, but both crimes were immensely profitable. *One of the most profitable days I've ever had*, Sandford thought.

Running Horse walked up to him. "Why you betray own people?" he asked.

"My only people, chief, is me," Sandford said. "The people you refer to never did anything for me. They couldn't care if I live or die. And I feel the same way about them." He looked toward his men. "Take good care of the horses, men. Don't you dare mistreat them. We got a big rancher down in

New Mexico who will pay top dollar for those steeds. And I do mean top dollar."

It shouldn't take long for us to make the trip down, Sandford thought. You could move horses a lot faster than cattle. He had wrangled herds before. Tough work but this time it was his herd. And he would get paid more than a hundred dollars a head at the end of the trail. He didn't know where Running Horse had gotten the three thousand dollars for the guns, and he didn't care.

He grinned. He had heard an army payroll had been stolen the previous week. No one knew who did it, because no man in the army patrol guarding it survived to tell the tale.

Three thousand, plus the thousand or so he would get from the herd. Down in New Mexico, Old Baron Knudson wanted the best horses for his ranch. The title of "baron" was a lie. Knudson didn't have any European royalty in his family. He had more kin among jackrabbits and wolves than he did among dukes and princes. But Sandford didn't care what his background was, as long as the man paid well.

All the Apaches were drinking now, and a few were galloping their horses as the liquor flowed. *That is a good way of getting your fool neck broken*, the outlaw thought. *You topple off a running horse while drunk, and it's easy to break bones.* He decided he and his outlaw band would leave promptly. Drunks can mistake friends for enemies. It might only be a matter of time until the Apaches started shooting at him and his men.

"Come on, fellas," he said. "Our business is over."

They herded the horses and headed them south. After he cashed in, he planned to take a long break, do some gambling, and buy drinks for every saloon girl in the place.

He smirked. *Besides*, he thought, *this would be a good time to get out of Colorado. Some blood-thirsty renegades just got some guns.*

~****~

Cully tied Samson to the hitching post outside the Durango sheriff's office and walked in. Two deputies sat at a desk playing cards. Jacob Salem, the one facing Cully, raised a finger to say hello.

"It must be a peaceful town if you two are playing cards," Cully said.

Salem nodded. "Last two weeks or so, it's been church social times. Very peaceful." He pointed to the jail cells. "We have no guests today, and we haven't for about two weeks. Don't know what got into people here, but everybody has been behavin' lately. Haven't even had any drunks."

"What can we do for you, Cully?" said Ben Haden, the second deputy.

"Nothing. Just came in to look over the wanted posters."

"Be our guest."

"Where's Sheriff Lassiter?"

"Comin' back on the train from Silverton, where he picked up a prisoner. Should be back this evening if you'd like to come back and say hello," Haden said.

"If I haven't found anything else to do, I might stick around a bit," Cully said as he grabbed the posters. He leaned against the wall and started going through the wanted list. He stopped at the second one. "Well, here's an ugly outlaw," he said.

"They're all ugly, Cully. Whereas deputies are handsome, outlaws always look like they've run through an ugly forest and hit every tree."

Cully chuckled, then a frown came over his face. He held up one poster. "Runnin' guns to Indians? That's a serious matter."

"You must be looking at Mel Sandford. Absolute gutter trash," Haden said. "There were several ranches attacked near Cortez a couple of days ago. Houses were burned down, horses stolen, nine people killed. Three of them were children. We believe Sandford supplied some Apaches with the weapons. Posse found some empty crates that held guns up near Mancos in Montezuma County. Sandford had been seen in the area, and he's known to deal with Indians."

"Nine dead," Cully said.

The crime angered his sense of justice. Some outlaws, even if they were on the wrong side of the law, had a degree of decency. Many had a code that they would not break. One of those codes was to not kill women or children. The thought disgusted Cully.

"Anyone know where this Sandford is now?" he said.

"Rumor is New Mexico. His crimes were in Colorado, and hear tell, a marshal from Pueblo who was in the area went looking for him. Haven't heard anything from him though."

Cully hung the posters back up on the wall. "Now might be a good time to ride down to New Mexico."

"Cully, there is never a good time to go to New Mexico. It's hot down there," Haden said.

Cully nodded. "And for one man in particular, it's going to get hotter." He tapped the poster. "He has a thousand-dollar bounty on his head. That makes the trip worthwhile, even with the hot weather. Please tell Sheriff Lassiter I said hello."

"We will."

As Cully walked toward the door, Salem's voice stopped him. "Cully, if you're going to look for Sandford, he's got a long scar on his right hand, below the knuckles. Someone scratched him with a knife. Scar like that would be difficult to hide."

Cully nodded. "Thanks for the tip." He walked outside and patted Samson. "Boy we're going on a little trip."

~****~

Later the next day, he crossed the state line into New Mexico. It was a big state, and he had been thinking about the best way to pick up Sandford's trail. Albuquerque was the largest city, and he knew it was easy to get lost in a big city. However, a large saloon had just opened in Gallup, and the town was getting a reputation as a gambling hub. Which meant money. Sandford might like poker. He might be feeling lucky since his dealings with the Apaches. After a score like that, a man would like a little fun. Gallup could be the place an outlaw would head.

Also, dealers tend to have sharp eyes. Perhaps they would notice a man with a long scar on his hand. It was as good a place as any to begin. Cully had money in the bank, so he had enough to qualify for any poker game.

When he entered Gallup after several days on the trail, he booked into a hotel and headed for the nearest restaurant for dinner. It was a very good meal, but the waiter hadn't seen any man with a long scar on his hand.

His next day at the saloon, he made some money but no success in finding Sandford. He discovered more than one poker player took a risk and bet on an inside straight even though the odds were not on their side. He won two hundred and fifty dollars before he quit playing. But whenever he asked about a man named Sandford with a scar on his hand, everybody shook their heads and said they didn't know him.

He sighed. He was used to action. But tracking down men often called for patience too. His father would occasionally note that patience was a virtue. And one of the hardest virtues to practice.

"The flesh is always impatient," the late Reverend Ben McCullough would say. "That's why it gets into trouble so often. It runs and acts before thinking. Patience will prevent a lot of problems."

Cully was sure that was true. As he walked back to his hotel, he smiled and told himself this was a time to develop patience. He also told himself that New Mexico was a large state. He couldn't expect to find an outlaw within the first week. But that was OK. It didn't matter if he had to spend two or three weeks or two or three months. He would find and bring Sandford to justice.

Any man who would sell guns and liquor to renegades didn't deserve to be walking the Earth. He needed to be in prison or in a grave.

Chapter 3

The sheriff of Gallup was a burly, round-eyed man with a bushy mustache curved over the edge of his lip. He had a tiny red scar over his right eyebrow. Cully thought the man had missed being in a grave by about an inch. He was used to dealing with both lawmen and outlaws. With his experience, he could size them up pretty quickly. He gave Sheriff Claude Broder high marks.

He wondered if the town fathers faced two choices. Hire a sheriff who looked the other way at the petty crimes brought by the gambling, allowing merchants to prosper. Or hire an honest man and gain a reputation that, although gambling was legal in the town, that not much else was. He thought the town had made the latter choice and Broder was hired to be the enforcer.

The sheriff scanned the poster which, admittedly, did not have a good sketch of Sandford on it.

"I haven't seen this man, Mr. Cully, although I will certainly keep my eye out for him. I served three years with the army. I've seen what happens when rebels get hold of liquor and guns. I buried a few people who were in the wrong place at the wrong time. When we put them in the ground, they were without their hair," he said.

Cully noted. "That's one reason I want to see this man hang."

"You said he's around here?"

"Rumor has it he headed for New Mexico after he finished his business in Colorado. I figured he might like to try his luck gambling."

"A lot of people do, and a lot of people end up broke." Broder picked up the poster. "I'll show this to all my deputies. Maybe we can spot him for you."

"I would appreciate that. I'll be roaming the saloons myself. But not looking for kings and queens. I'm looking for Sandford."

Broder leaned back in his chair. "The thing is, we always have new people coming in to gamble, and they keep coming in. It's going to be tough spotting him in a town like this. I don't know if you have any specific plan in mind..."

"Only the most basic plan there is. Spread money around and ask people if they've seen him. Promise them a reward if they know where he is."

"That may work, but it also might tip Sandford off that you're looking for him. Bad as he is, I imagine he has a few friends around here."

"The only friends he has are the ones money can buy. But that's fine. If he knows I'm after him and wants to try to stop me, I'm ready. If he figures he better run, I'll pick up his trail. There are few people better at tracking than I am. I figure if he's out in the wild, the odds are on my side."

"From what you say, he has some money. Maybe he bought himself some protection."

"That's fine too," Cully said, smiling.

~****~

At a back table at the Lonestar Saloon, a man named Jake Sutton reached across and pulled more than four hundred dollars in chips his way. He wore a big smile and almost laughed as he pulled the money toward him. He would have laughed, but he knew, at times, discretion was valuable when playing poker. The men who were scowling because they lost would not appreciate being mocked. So Sutton kept smiling and placed a blue chip on the tray of the waiter who brought him a drink.

One of the irritated men was Sandford. He took a cigar out of his coat pocket and angrily bit into it. He flicked a match and brought the flame to the tobacco while starring at Sutton. "You're getting' mighty lucky," he said, almost growling instead of speaking.

"Luck has nothing to do with it. You calculate and make an intelligent decision. If you rely on luck, my friend, you lose," Sutton said.

"I ain't your friend."

"You are ridin' a lucky streak," said Roy Newcom, another man at the table. He had a bunch of bushy hair and a thick mustache.

"Which I trust will last a few more hands. Players get upset, they lose, but may I remind you that I didn't deal that hand. The cards came to me," Sutton said, keeping his smile.

Ronnie Branson, the fourth man at the table, picked up the deck. "I'm dealing this hand, and you won't get any luck from me. Ante up."

All the players pushed fifty-dollar chips onto the center of the table. Sandford's scowl didn't change when he picked up his cards.

"It's to you, Sutton," Branson said.

Sutton tossed a hundred dollars into the pot. "Let's go for high stakes this time," he said.

Several men shook their heads. But Sandford and Branson called.

"How many cards?" Branson asked, picking up the deck.

"None. I'll stay with those." Sutton said.

Sandford's eyes clicked with anger. "You're bluffing. I can smell a bluff a mile away."

"Each man plays his own game, friend, but I suggest you don't make poker decisions based on your nose. That never works out."

As if to reply, Sandford counted out two hundred dollars in chips and tossed them toward the center of the table. He grabbed a stack of bills and counted out another hundred. "I'll call you and raise," he said.

Branson tapped his cards on the table. He frowned. "I'm playing with some high rollers. I've noticed sometimes luck will shift in a game. I wonder if it's on your side now, Mr. Sutton."

"There's only way to find out."

Branson tapped the cards again, then reached for his stack of cash. "Against my better judgement," he said. "But I am curious."

"I'll stand," Sutton said.

"I won't," Sandford replied. "I told you I can smell a bluff." He tossed two hundred more dollars into the pot. "Call or back down."

Sutton just smiled and matched Sandford's bid. "What do you have?"

Sandford slapped cards on the table. "I've got three good-looking ladies. Beat that!"

Sutton almost yawned his reply. "OK," he said. In languid, casual movements, he laid a king of hearts on the table, then the king of clubs, and finally the king of diamonds.

At first, shock rose in Sandford's face, then anger came as his nostrils flared. "You lyin', cheatin' polecat."

Sutton eased his hand toward his holster, feeling the coolness of his gun with his fingers. For a second, he thought he might have to trade bullets with Sandford. Then a well-dressed man eased up to his opponent.

"Any trouble here?" he asked. Bart Armstrong helped with security in the casino. He was strong and fast and had a reputation.

Sandford glared at him but lifted his hand away from his gun and put it on the table. He took a deep breath. "No trouble," he said.

"Perhaps you need to step away from the game for a few minutes," Armstrong said. "This is a good time for that. Mr. Murdock would like to see you in his office."

Sandford knew Murdock ran the gambling house. They were not friends but had done occasional favors for one another. The owner cared nothing about his outlaw background.

"Let me escort you," Armstrong said.

Sandford stood up and let himself be guided into Murdock's office. He eased down in a chair facing the desk. Armstrong shut the door on his way out.

"What did you want to see me about?" Sandford said. He gave a surly smile.

"You should be more pleasant. I'm doin' you a big favor."

"How do you figure that?"

"Because you have a man looking for you who is spending money to make sure he finds you."

Sandford's eyes blinked alertness. His muscles tensed. "How do you know that?"

"Because he offered money to one of my bartenders for information. Gave your name and had a poster on you. Fifty dollars. That's a lot of money for bartenders. Fortunately, Jake said he hadn't seen anyone who looked like you. I made up for Jake's loss when I gave him fifty dollars as appreciation for his silence. I don't like to lose customers, and you're a customer."

"You get the guy's name?"

"Cully. He goes by one name, I guess. Kind of like 'Earp' or 'Holliday' or 'Hickock.' There are some men who only need one name."

Sandford shook his head. "Whoever he is, he's not in their league. I never heard of him."

"You better give him your attention. One of the deputies here is my friend. Well, maybe not a friend, but let's say we trade information at times. I asked him about Cully. Found out he's a first-rate bounty hunter, who also doubles at times as a deputy marshal on occasion. He's tough, and he's good with a gun. He's walked a lot of outlaws into sheriffs' offices. He's also put more than one in a grave. You better be careful."

"I don't know why he's on my tail."

"Maybe due to the bounty on your head. How much is it? A thousand?"

"About that, the last time I checked. But that's up in Colorado. I'm not wanted in New Mexico."

"You are by at least one person. I just wanted you to know about Cully. I suggest you get out and find a place to cool your heels."

"Maybe."

"If you stay, Cully will probably find you, and if there's a shootout, even if you win, other lawmen and bounty hunters might take notice. You might want to go think about this, but don't cause any trouble on your way out, ya hear?

~****~

Sandford walked out of the office but paused at the swinging doors of the saloon. He looked both ways, up and down the street, before he stepped out. Although he didn't know why. He didn't know what Cully looked like. He wouldn't know the man if he walked past him and said good morning. He walked down to his hotel and went up to his second-floor room that looked out on the street. A bottle stood on the desk. He took it and pulled out the cork. He eased down on the edge of the bed and took a long swig of the whiskey.

His first instinct was to stay in town and let Cully find him. He had bested other men. However, what Murdock said was true. If there was a gunfight, the rumors would begin that he was a fugitive. Local law would get wind of the fact he sold whiskey to those Apaches, and that would make the town inhospitable to him. Not only bounty hunters and lawmen but random strangers might seek him out to kill. Some man might have lost a friend or relative in an Indian raid. Unlike a lawman, that individual would not give him any warning or tell him to throw down his guns. He'd just be gunned in the back.

He took another drink from the bottle.

So a short hiatus might be the best choice. Lawman or bounty hunter, whoever was hunting him, couldn't stay forever. The man would have to return to Colorado, eventually. He could go out in the country, relax, and do some hunting before returning to town. Or simply just leave and not return. Find another town and take up residence. Maybe even head toward Texas. He had plenty of money. And he had always wanted to see Texas.

Of course there was another method. If the man called Cully was hunting him, he could find Cully first and kill him. That took care of any worries. There was an element of danger, but he could handle it. But he had to do it secretly. He did not want to be connected to a shooting. The law would start asking questions, and he didn't want his background known. *People have that irrational prejudice against running guns to Indians. A few might want to lynch me if the truth became known.* He nodded. It was safer to leave Gallup for a while. Let the bounty hunter find nothing and go back to Colorado. Then he would be safe and be able to put his past behind him.

But... he did not like having a hound dog hunter on his trail. That was dangerous, too. Such a man could show up at any time. Sandford didn't like looking over his shoulder. That was one reason he headed for New Mexico after his latest, and very profitable, transaction with the Apaches. It lessened the chances of a lone wolf hunter. Why would any

Colorado bounty hunter track him to another state when there were plenty of outlaws in that state?

He had cigars on the small desk in the room. He picked one up and lit it. He took another glance out the window. He knew he had to be careful. Being an outlaw for years, he had some knowledge about bounty hunters. Some worked in pairs. That was understandable because they were tracking down murderers. There was a degree of safety in numbers. But the solitary hunters were like a Colorado panther. They hunted alone and were deadly in tracking their prey.

He snorted, as if reacting to a knife stabbing his side. At first, the name Cully didn't ring a bell. But now he remembered. He had heard the name. Man was linked with another bounty hunter from Denver, a man whose name had slipped out of his mind. Both were the best in the business, he had been told. You'd rather have a pack of jackals on your trail than Cully. Yes, now he remembered. The son of a preacher man. The conversation mentioning Cully had taken place two, maybe three, years ago. At that time, he paid it no mind. But now it came back to him. That changed the situation.

Cully might not give up.

He spit out a speck of tobacco.

To go up against a man like Cully, he might need help. He was never one for a fair fight.

Chapter 4

It didn't take long for him to find Reed McKinney, one of the men who had been in his outlaw band. McKinney was dependable. The two had formed a friendship, or as much as a friendship as two outlaws can have. The two sat in a saloon across a circular table. McKinney was a tall, tanned man who had deep-set dark eyes. He wasn't much for talking but he could shoot straight and toss a knife with unfailing accuracy. The bartender had put a bottle on the table and two glasses in front of the men.

Sandford lifted his glass, half full of whiskey. "Thanks for coming, Reed."

McKinney gave a slight nod. "Say what you've got to say."

"It turns out I might need a little help. I may have a lawman on my tail. I've never met him, but I hear he's like a mountain lion. He hunts with the best of them and brings in his prey both dead and alive, mostly dead."

"Who is he?"

"A man named Cully."

McKinney took a sip of his drink. "Heard the name. Said to be a straight-shooter. And a good one. Heard he's as good as Holliday, without the cough."

"No, don't think Cully is sick. I wish he was, but he's full of good health and whiskey. Since he's after me, I figure I could use a gun or two."

"Or three or four," McKinney said. "But I don't see two or three people around this here table. I just see me."

"Other members of our gang are who knows where. You're the only man I can trust." Sandford drained his glass then grabbed the bottle and refilled it. "I don't expect you to volunteer. You're taking a risk taking on Cully. Five hundred dollars for your help. I can give you two fifty now and the rest when Cully's dead."

"Five hundred." McKinney paused a moment. "Sounds good. Seven fifty sounds better."

Sandford almost choked on his drink. "Seven fifty! Reed, we're friends."

"Friendship only goes so far. Would you take a risk for me for anything less? We may be friends, but neither of us are sentimental. It's a hard life, and we make hard choices. When all is chewed up and spit out, each man stands alone. He has to look after himself."

He paused and took out a wad of tobacco. He bit off a piece of it. He chewed while talking. Sandford just stared at him while gritting his teeth.

"Now, possibly, you could take Cully. Or Cully might take you. I'd say the odds were pretty even, with a slight edge to the bounty hunter 'cause this is his job. He's experienced at it." McKinney still had the tobacco in his hand.

He pointed it at Sandford. "So if you want an advantage, it would be wise to take on a partner. We made a lot of money with the Apaches, but that won't do you no good under a tombstone. Seven fifty ain't much compared to the rest of your life... now is it?" He stuck the wad back into his pocket. "I may come across hard, but you know if I give you my word, I won't run out on you. I won't take the money and run."

Sandford thought for a minute then nodded. "I'll take the deal."

"I figure maybe you thought I'd take five hundred, so you brought half. So I will accept that. You can pay the rest when Cully is pushing up daisies. What do you need me to do?"

"As for right now, you follow when I leave town and see if anyone comes after me. If so and you get a clear chance to put a bullet in him, you do so. Don't waste an opportunity. Don't rush. Make sure you can take a clear shot. I'll be looking for a place to ambush him myself. One of us should be able to get him."

~****~

As he walked out of the saloon, Sandford was angry at the money he had to lay out, but he knew it went with the territory of being an outlaw. When you are on the run, everything you need to buy comes at a higher price. He also knew an outlaw had no real friends. It was one of Jesse James's own gang members that killed him. There wasn't a lot of loyalty on the other side of the law. Still, he had found a partner. McKinney would not betray him. He liked to think of himself as a brave man, but he felt more secure with McKinney working with him.

Tomorrow morning. Before sunup. Saddle up and ride out of town. The terrain was rugged heading southeast toward Albuquerque. A man would have to ride through a forest then deal with rocky ground for miles. On that type of trail, Sandford knew he could tell if he was being followed... and he or his partner could take care of the pursuer without any problem. Leave him dead on the ground and let the buzzards have him.

First, he had to make sure Cully was on his trail. He nodded. He knew how he could do that. The good news was, after killing Cully, he would be in the clear. He'd keep traveling until he arrived in Texas. Then he could put his past behind him and enjoy the money.

~***~

Cully was eating breakfast the next morning when he noticed the stranger walk toward his table. It didn't cause him any alarm. In his profession, he had grown to read people. The man wasn't hostile. He wasn't walking over to fight. So Cully wondered what he wanted. He picked up a strip of bacon and took a bite out of it. The man was taller than most other men. Slender but not skinny. He had black hair and a thin, black mustache.

The man stopped at the table. "You Cully?" he asked.

"Yep."

"You're the one asking about a man called Sandford."

"Sure am. A hundred dollars if you know where he is," Cully said.

"I know where he used to be, may not be there now. But it's a place you might find him."

Cully eased back in his chair. "Sounds good enough." He pulled money from his shirt and counted out several bills and put them on the table. "There's fifty. If the information is good, you get fifty more."

The cowboy nodded. "I don't know where Sandford is now, but he's staying at the Brazos Hotel. Been there about a week."

Cully smiled. He judged the man as honest. He pulled out more bills and handed them over. "Thank you."

"Heard a rumor he was selling guns to Indians. That true?"

Cully nodded. "Yes."

"Then he should be hanged," the man said, a menacing tone in his voice.

Cully swallowed the last bit of bacon. "I agree completely."

Cully paid his bill and told the clerk it was a very good breakfast. The Brazos Hotel was only about five blocks away, so he headed down the street. The day was sunny with only a few clouds in the sky. He nodded at several other walkers. He eased his hand on his gun. He hoped Sandford was at the hotel. If he wasn't, he figured he'd have a long chase before he captured the outlaw. Perhaps that chase would be shortened considerably.

He opened the door to the hotel and walked up to the counter. A short, chubby man smiled at him. His features indicated that Cully walking into the establishment was the high point of his day. *If Sandford is here, it will be the high point of my day too*, Cully thought.

"Yes, sir, what can I do for you? Like a room?"

"No, I'd like to see one of your guests. Do you have a Mel Sandford staying here?"

"We did, sir, but he checked out this morning. Very early."

Cully didn't change his expression, hiding his disappointment. "Were you here when he checked out?"

"Yes, this was my day to take the early shift. But we always have a few guests who like to leave early. Some want to take off before dawn."

"Did Sandford say where he was heading?"

The clerk nodded. He kept the enthusiasm in his voice. "As a matter of fact, he did. Said he was heading over to Grants Camp. You know, that was kinda strange. He mentioned his destination three times. Grants."

Cully raised his eyebrows. "Three times?"

"Yes, sir. Most of our customers just leave. I didn't ask where he was going. Just said I hoped he liked his stay and wished him a good trip."

Cully picked up a dollar from his shirt and gave it to the clerk. "Thank you. You've been very hopeful."

"Thank you, sir!"

Cully turned around, walked out of the hotel and stood just outside. He paused, rolled a cigarette, and lit it. As a slight wind swirled the dust in the street, he scratched his jaw.

"Now why would a man on the run tell a hotel clerk where he was going and tell him three times?" Cully asked the air. "That's odd behavior. And stupid behavior. Sandford may be a lot of things, but he's not stupid."

He stepped out into the street. His father had taught him chess, and he enjoyed the game. However, he noticed that while it demanded skill and intelligence, there was an oddity in the game that was not in life. In chess, there was no luck, no accidents. A player made all the moves. If he missed something, it was his own fault. If he lost, he had no one to blame but himself.

He thought Mel Sandford might be playing chess with him and had just made his opening move. He could think of one reason why a wanted man might advertise his intentions. He knew someone was tracking him and Sandford would be watching for the tracker.

"A chess game. You have invited me to a chess game of life and death," Cully said.

He puffed on the cigarette watched the wind blow the smoke away.

"I accept."

At the stable, he saddled Samson, filled his saddle bags with the grub he'd bought, and bought an extra canteen that he filled with water. He liked two canteens, especially if he was traveling in an area he wasn't familiar with. No man wanted to be caught without water in a strange land. He had to think about Samson too. A horse was given water before his rider. If a horse went down, his rider was as good as dead.

When riding, Cully knew he didn't move with any haste. He didn't think Sandford was moving swiftly. He would travel at average speed and watch for the rider behind him. Cully lifted the binoculars from the package he bought at the general store and wound the string around his saddle horn. He figured the binoculars would be of great use on the journey. Seven miles from Gallup, the trail led into a forest. There were plenty of places for Sandford to hide and shoot at a tracker. He put his boot into the stirrup and lifted himself into the saddle.

"Let's view some country, Samson. It might be a scenic trail."

The moment the line was out of his mouth, he realized there would be blood at the end of it.

~****~

Clouds began forming and reforming as Cully rode out from the town. The longer Samson trotted down the road, the darker the sky became. Cully frowned. He was told it didn't rain all that much in New Mexico. As he looked at the darkening clouds, he thought he might have been lied to. The air had changed and now smelled like rain. He didn't mind rain. Someone out on the range wanted to kill him. It's more difficult to take good aim when rain is pounding you and you're soaking wet.

Cully watched the trail. He knew his prey had ridden this way. He made out one set of hoofprints that led toward the forest. Faint but the lines in the dust were there. Then he spied something else.

He halted Samson and climbed down. As he bent down to the dusty road, the first drops of rain plopped to the ground, leaving damp marks. Three or four brown drops in the tan soil. Cully reached for the object and picked it up. A tobacco pouch, now empty. A rider had emptied it and tossed it aside. Not a wise move if an outlaw thinks he's being followed. He stuffed the pouch in his pants pocket. He didn't like to see trash in the forests and valleys, anyway. He looked around. There was no sure way of knowing the pouch belonged to Sandford. He believed the outlaw was traveling southeast, and the pouch was found on the trail. That was a clue, but it didn't mean Sandford dropped it. *But sometimes if you lack conclusive proof*, Cully thought, *you have to go on a hunch.* He climbed on Samson again and spurred the horse on.

"You know what I think, Samson," he said. He often talked to his mount. Usually a horse was the only one a solitary rider could talk to. "I think our gun runner got a whiff that a bounty hunter or lawman might be tracking him. So he took off but basically left a message with the hotel clerk about where he'd be going. Now why would he do that? He wanted to place the tracker, if there was one. When he knew a rider was coming, he would lie in wait to kill the man. Better to surprise the tracker than to have the tracker surprise him."

Samson keep trotting on the road but said nothing.

"All in all, I'd say it's a good plan, if it turns out well." He sat and listened to the clomp of Samson's hooves. "But it's not going to turn out well," he said.

He turned and came into sight of a burbling brook. He eased Samson over to it and let the horse drink. Always take advantage of brooks and streams. You never know when you will see the next one. It was a rule he always followed. He leaned on his saddle horn.

Now where will that heathen polecat attempt the ambush? he thought. First, he had to make sure there is, actually, a man following him. Then he could decide on the location. In his own county, Cully knew he could guess where the attack might come, giving him a chance to sneak up on the gunman. But in a state he didn't know, he was at a disadvantage. And he couldn't make any mistakes. Not in this game.

He thought for a moment and pulled out the small map he had made. He opened it and studied his markings. He wondered if he could circle around and possibly come out behind Sandford. Then the man would be riding into his trap. His finger traced the forest. Due to the curvature of the land, that would not be easy. Plus about halfway into the forest, two trails broke away from the one he was traveling now. He couldn't know which one Sandford would take. It was better just to track him. Be very careful but track him.

Chapter 5

Since dawn, McKinney had camped a few miles outside of Gallup. He was about a half mile from the road but could see riders. He sat with a pan over his campfire cooking bacon and potatoes. He wasn't in any hurry. Sandford had said not to be. Take time to make sure of your target and make sure you get a good shot at him. He glanced toward the road and turned over a strip of sizzling bacon. In this part of the state, there couldn't be too many riders going to Grants. There might be a number of people heading to Gallup but not many going to Grants. He had time for breakfast.

He glanced at his rifle. But he wasn't going to use it here. This spot was too close to town. He wanted a more isolated section. So when the man fell from his saddle he wouldn't be discovered for days or even weeks.

He stiffened when he saw a rider coming from Gallup. Then he eased. The man was chubby, dressed fancy, but didn't ride well. He didn't rest easy on the horse. Looked like some type of salesman. McKinney shook his head. The man definitely was not a bounty hunter or lawman.

You could tell a man of the West. He was almost one with his horse. Cowboys knew the value of such animals and took care of them. If his horse appeared to be aching, his owner was immediately attentive. The cowboy felt the same way about his gun. He wanted it cleaned and ready. Especially in this country.

It was rumored there were renegade Apaches near here. In that case, a rider better have a ready horse and a ready gun. If not, he was dead. McKinney forked the bacon and the potatoes and put them on a plate.

It was true that two drunken men at a saloon had told him of the renegade Apaches, so he couldn't be sure of the truth of the story. But the region was inhabited by members of the tribe. They had roamed it for years. A man always had to be careful. That's how he kept alive. Of course, he was on good terms with some Apaches. But he doubted the rebels he had dealt with in Colorado had passed the word down to their cousins that he was a friend. Plus, he didn't have guns or liquor with him this trip.

He ate the bacon and potatoes while watching the road. Another man passed by, but after watching him for a moment, McKinney shrugged. He guessed the man was a cowhand, heading back to his ranch. The man didn't have the cold steadiness that a bounty hunter would have. He forked a potato and went back to eating.

It wasn't bad money. Seven hundred and fifty dollars for a few days or maybe a week of work. Working with Sandford was profitable. McKinney admitted that. The pay for the guns and liquor exceeded his expectations and most of the credit went to Sandford. He doubted it was easy dealing with Apache renegades. He was glad he didn't have to do it. But Sandford seemed a natural at it.

Pity they were not still up in Colorado. Sandford could probably get those Apaches to take care of this man Cully.

He heard good things about the bounty hunter, but even a man such as Cully could not defeat a few dozen men alone.

McKinney grabbed his canteen and washed down his breakfast. As he lowered it, he spied the tall, brown man riding by. He didn't have a clear view of him. Trees hindered his vision. The horse weaved back and forth among the oaks and aspens. McKinney focused on the rider. There was a man of the West. The man seemed at home on a horse, and he rode a good one. Even at a distance, McKinney knew the mount was a fine piece of horse flesh. He rode with confidence. He could just barely make out the man's smile. He had seen a few such men before. As an outlaw, when he did spot them, he turned and walked the other way. No sense looking for trouble.

He twisted the cap back on his canteen then lifted it to his saddle horn. No hurry. He'd be patiently tracking the man waiting for an opening.

He snickered. He would be behind the man, and Sandford would be in front of him. No matter Cully's reputation, the man would soon have to prove just how good he was.

He slipped his hand onto the handle of his knife. He eased it out of his sheath, then eased it back in. He carried two knives. He was good with them. He believed no one could defeat him in a knife fight. He could throw each of his knives with accuracy too. He was almost as quick as a good man with a gun. That's why he preferred knife fights. He was deadly close in with an opponent. He had killed more than one man with a knife and was prepared to kill more. Cully might be good with guns, but if he could get him one on one, knife to knife, the odds would be on his side, McKinney thought.

~****~

Six miles ahead, Sandford, a cigar in his mouth, looked over his shoulders at the trees and trail. He then told himself looking back was silly. Even if he was being followed, the thick forest would hide the tracker. He turned his horse around so he could look back on the trail without turning his head. He didn't even know Cully. He wouldn't recognize the man if he walked up and slapped him. But he was uneasy the man might be on his trail. The bits and pieces he had heard about Cully made him cautious... and just a bit fearful.

He sighed and could feel the tension in his body. He felt in his saddle bag for the bottle of whiskey he brought with him. His teeth bit into the cork and pulled it out. He rolled the cork around on his fingers while taking a large gulp. He didn't like feeling edgy. He had been in dangerous situations and always came out alive. He shook himself. But in all those situations, he had never been this edgy. Maybe he was just upset at losing that last poker hand.

If he was nervous, then the sooner he killed Cully the better. He looked around again. He needed some high ground, but he didn't know this territory. High ground so he could peer out and see if anyone was following. If so, he could lay a trap.

What he wasn't going to do was ride up to Cully and challenge him. Sandford didn't mind a fair fight, if there wasn't any other way. But the odds on a fair fight were even. He didn't like that. He wanted the odds on his side. Ambushing a man heightened the chances for survival. There was no reason to stand face to face with a bounty hunter if you could shoot him in the back. Simple logic. The first option had an element of risk. The second did not. Never take a risk you didn't have to was one of Sandford's rules. It had served him well.

He turned his horse back around and spurred it. The only thing to do was keep riding and look for the high ground that would give him an advantage. As he puffed on his cigar, he thought again that he didn't know what Cully looked like. If he saw a rider, how would he know it was the bounty hunter? He had to take that risk. Rather, the unidentified rider would have to take the risk. He wasn't going to wave at any rider and ask, "By the way, is your name Cully?" Cully had one advantage on him. The hunter knew what he looked like. He had a wanted poster with Sandford's likeness on it. Wasn't a good likeness, but it was good enough.

Sandford eyed the forest. He wondered if there was any place he could hide in safety and wait for his hunter. He would look for one as he rode. He lifted the cigar from his mouth and spat tobacco juice on the ground. That was the one bad thing about being an outlaw. You're always on the run.

But not when he got to Texas. No posters on him in Texas. Nobody knew him there. He'd be safe in the Lone Star State.

As he rode, in the distance he saw elevated ground. That might be his chance. It wasn't a high elevation. In fact, it looked like the ground tumbled into a gully. But the two sides of the gully rose about thirty feet above the stream that ran through it. Scrub and bushes and a few trees alongside it. A nice place to rest a few minutes from a long ride. Had shade and a stream. At least that's how it looked from a distance. Might be the place. If he could find a good location on the higher ground. When Cully rode into the gully, a good marksman should be able to take a clean shot at him. Sandford knew he wasn't an expert marksman, but he wasn't an awful shot either. He squinted his eyes to see better.

At the back edge of the gully, he found a satisfactory place. The ground dipped on his part of the trail. But the banks were almost four feet high. He rode past it looking for a good hiding spot. Fifty yards past the gully, a band of trees spread across the plain. One tall oak stood over the rest. Sandford rode to it and looked up. The branches should support him. He glanced over the limbs and branches and thought he found a good spot. He pulled his rifle from his scabbard, swung his left leg over his horse and eased onto the tree.

In two quick movements, he found what he was looking for. He could sit on the branch with a degree of stability. The tree looked down on the gully. He should be able to get a good shot at Cully. It was the best chance he had with the type of land he had to deal with. He pulled his rifle up and aimed. Then nodded. He had a clear shot. Not much cover in the gully if a shootout was necessary. Cully would be pinned down and not expecting an ambush. Cully would probably figure his prey was galloping toward Grants.

Fine.

Sandford figured he could kill Cully before the man knew what hit him.

Just in case, he walked his horse back to the gully and let him drink. Then returned to the tree. He sat down in its shade. He didn't know how long it would take for the tracker to reach him. But he figured Cully was first rate. So it wouldn't be long before he reached the gully. Which, for him, would be a cemetery.

Chapter 6

Cully slowed Samson down as they rode around a curve. He stared down at the ground as he halted the horse. No one else would have cared what was on the ground, but he did. The rider must have stopped under two large pine trees. Several small bushes had grown together, forming a hedge between the trees. The hedge basically protecting a small area from the wind. That would explain the ashes on the road. Cigar ashes. Three large clumps of them. Cully thought the rider must have eased down from his horse for a few minutes, maybe just to have a smoke. Horse droppings stretched in a line not far from the ashes. A horse and rider had definitely come this way.

Rain drops plunked on the ground. He had expected a downpour, but the rain was slow and steady. One drop hit a pile of ash and collapsed it.

Since this was a place for smoking, Cully took his tobacco from his pocket and rolled a cigarette. Fact number one: there was a rider on the road and, from all indications, the rider came from Gallup. Fact number two: outlaw Sandford had departed from Gallup that very morning. Fact number three: New Mexico is not a booming area the way San Francisco was after the gold strike in '49. Not that many booming towns in New Mexico. You can ride for miles without seeing anyone. And on a back trail, how many people could you expect? Sort of narrowed down the odds. So Cully, puffing out tobacco smoke, thought the man he was trailing must be Sandford.

He had been wondering. The signs could point to a random rider. Now he thought it must be Sandford. Sometimes you have to go with hunches, and that was his hunch. But Sandford also suspected someone might be tailing him. Would he run for the border? Or lay a trap?

Cully considered that question. He leaned toward the latter. If Sandford had a posse after him, he might ride day and night to find a place of safety. But if it were just one man, he might fight it out.

"I'll have to remember that as I ride," Cully said as he lifted himself back into the saddle. "Now where would be a good place for an ambush?"

~***~

The few drops of rain hadn't increased but hadn't diminished either. The sky was in a constant state of dripping water without raining. He rode easily, humming a song about his days punching cattle. Several minutes later, he pulled out his binoculars and looked into the distance.

A gully. The forest cleared a bit, and the trail led into a gully. Water dripped on the binoculars and his face as he stared. Everything looked peaceful. He saw no men or animals. He eased the binoculars down and gave a deep sigh.

"Looks peaceful, but I need to be careful. Wouldn't you agree, Samson?"

Samson neighed and nodded. Cully knew the horse could understand only a few words, but he seemed to understand the tone of Cully's voice. He would nod or shake his head in response. He had noticed Samson had picked up a slight limp. Might be nothing to worry about, but he wanted to check it. The gully would be a good place for that.

The rain's pitter-patter on the leaves irritated him for some reason. He shifted in the saddle. He lifted his pistol from his holster then eased it back in.

"Let's go, Samson," he said. "But let's go slowly."

Samson trotted forward. Cully looked back and forth, without nervousness. The rain had mucked the light tracks. If any had headed for the gully, they had been erased by the rain. No ashes or tobacco pouches either. He glanced at the trees behind the gully and saw nothing but brown branches and green leaves. Samson's hooves clumped on the soft, now slightly muddy, road.

~***~

In the distance, Sandford tensed. The man approaching had to be Cully. He was lucky he could deal with him sooner than later. He eased his finger onto the trigger even though the target wasn't in range yet. And he was riding slowly, carefully. Sandford checked his position. He thought he was completely hidden by the brush and limbs. With the rifle barrel, he eased a small branch over to the side so he could see better. From his angle, it wasn't an easy shot—very little was easy in the West—but it was a makeable one. He wanted Cully closer. The closer a man was, the easier to kill him.

Cully eased Samson down into the gully. The ground was muddier, but it didn't slow up Samson's gait. The small brook ran swiftly across the space, rippling as it flowed. Cully eased down as Samson tilted his head to drink.

"Get on the other side of your horse," Sandford growled to himself.

Cully stood on the far side of Samson. The horse blocked the outlaw from getting a clear shot. As the rain dropped on the leaves, Sandford cursed. He couldn't get a good target. Cully's head and shoulders were able to be seen and not much more. Such a small target from such a long way... He shook his head. He lowered his rifle, cursing again.

He hoped Cully would move around his horse, but Cully patiently stayed where he was. He took his canteen and refilled it with water, still blocked by his horse. Sandford gritted his teeth. He was not a patient man. A thought hit him to get it over with now. Fire at the man and the horse. Kill them both if he needed to. His arms tensed, and he raised the rifle again, angry enough to fire. At the last second, he drew it back.

"Don't make mistakes," he growled under his breath. "One shot is all you need. Don't mess it up." He took a deep breath and kept watching.

Cully hung his canteen back on his saddle horn. He patted Samson. The rain increased slightly. The drops increased their patter on the ground and in the brook. Sandford nervously wiped his hands on his shirt. His hands were getting wet, the last thing a shooter wanted. He looked away for a second trying to find a dry place on his shirt.

He tensed and grabbed the rifle again as Cully walked around his horse. Sandford lifted the rifle. Tensed his muscles. As he squeezed the trigger, Cully slipped in the mud and tumbled on the wet ground. The fall knocked him to the side, enough that the bullet missed his chest but grazed his shoulder. As soon as he hit the ground, he rolled quickly to the side. Two bullets plunked into the wet sand beside him. Cully leaped up and raced to his horse. He grabbed his rifle as another bullet whizzed past his ear. *Damn, he's quick,* Sandford thought. *Never seen a man faster. Moves like lightning.*

Cully ran and threw himself against the bank of the gully. The angle of the land gave him a degree of cover. He had seen a whiff of smoke. He raised his rifle and fired.

Two leaves were knocked from a branch near Sandford. The man shook with fury as he stared at the now partially hidden Cully. He raised his rifle again, but the limb wavered. He slipped on the wet branch. He lifted a hand from the rifle and grabbed another branch to steady himself. As he did, a bullet skimmed over his back. He groaned as the pain hit him. A trail of blood ran from the wound. Sandford knew the wound wasn't serious, but it was annoying and would slow down his movements.

In the distance, McKinney heard the shots and galloped toward them. He whipped the reins forward and back on his horse's back. This was the time to catch Cully in a crossfire, and he didn't want to waste it. As he rode, he pulled his rifle out. From the sound, he thought he'd be at the scene of the shooting in a few minutes.

Another of Cully's bullets split a branch a few feet from Sandford. Cully had gotten a bead on him, so Sandford jumped down from the tree, causing more pain to shoot from his wound. He fired back but knew his fire didn't come close to the man. He turned around but couldn't see his adversary. He fired again and thought he could keep Cully pinned down. He hoped the shooting got the attention of McKinney. If so, soon the battle would be two against one. He wondered if he had wounded Cully. He thought so, but the man gave no indication of being shot. *Bullet couldn't have hit him in the leg. He moved too fast for that.* Sandford hid in the shadow of the tree and scanned the gully. He didn't see Cully. He spit and cursed. He should have killed the man. Dang bad luck. He peered beyond the tree again, looking for any trace of the bounty hunter.

Cully had raced over to the other side of the gully while Sandford climbed down from the tree. He felt the blood slide down his sleeve. Only a small trickle though. He had experienced more serious wounds and wasn't concerned about it. But he was concerned the outlaw had him trapped. From his position, Sandford looked down at the gully and at the open space. The bank of the gully gave him a degree of protection, but it he couldn't charge the gunman or work his way toward him because there was no cover. If he moved, he'd be an easy target, unless his bullet had hit the outlaw's gun hand. He'd have to wait until he could get a clean shot.

The rain plodded against his head and body, wetting his shirt. He blinked and could barely make out some shadows against a tree in the distance. Not clear enough for a clean shot. A standoff. He aimed his rifle and, when ready, squeezed the trigger twice. One bullet skimmed off wood, and he saw the man or the man's shadow duck. A rifle was swung up and fired back, but the bullets angled left of Cully.

Cully looked at Samson. One plan would be to leap on Samson, ride out of range, and circle around, possible getting into a better position. A plan, he thought, but not necessarily a good plan. The ground was now muddy, making it more difficult for Samson to get traction. Once he did, he'd be fine. But Samson was a big target. What if Sandford decided to shoot the horse instead of the rider? Cully would be stranded. Plus, he didn't want to lose Samson. A cowboy had to be mindful of his horse as well as himself. Samson was almost totally covered by the bank and Cully wanted to keep his horse out of the line of fire. He didn't think Sandford was a great shot, but anyone could hit a horse. And if he did, he wouldn't even have to hang around to trade bullets. He could just ride out knowing Cully was stranded.

So why didn't he?

The thought startled Cully. He looked back at Samson, bent down, and rushed the five steps to his mount and pulled him closer to the sand bank. He patted him. He checked the elevation of the bank and the height of Samson. About the same. Yet the outlaw hadn't tried to take out Samson. For a moment, that was puzzling to Cully. Sandford didn't care anything about shooting humans. He certainly wouldn't care about shooting a horse if it helped his getaway.

Maybe his mind was on something else...

Cully turned slowly and looked behind him. As he did, a gray rider came into view in the distance. As Cully watched, the man grabbed his rifle and brought it up to his shoulder and aimed it.

Lightning flashed, ripping the sky with a streak of white. Possibly due to his wet hands or his mount's minor stumble, the rifle slipped from the rider's hand. It fell to the muddy ground below. That didn't stop the gunman. He spurred his horse faster. In the rain, Cully stepped back, confused. The rider was less than ten yards away but hadn't pulled a gun. Was he going to just ride by?

Then with a quickness that surprised him, the man whipped out a knife. As his horse rode past Cully, he leaped from the saddle, knife in hand, and landed on Cully, knocking him back into the mud. Cully tossed the man off and quickly stood up, pulling out his own knife. McKinney lunged toward him, but Cully batted the knife away.

Sandford had watched his partner make the charge. He couldn't see the fight, only the tops of the men's heads, but he knew this might be his chance. He pulled his gun and ran towards them. He was so anxious, his boots slipped on the mud, and he sprawled on the ground. He yelled with pain as the fall sent jolts of pain through his back. He sank a knee to the muddy ground and pulled himself up, groaning. He half-stumbled toward the fight. His back ached with every step.

After three steps, he stopped. Rain now poured over him, drenching his clothes and hair. Even so, for a second, he stood still in the rain. Then he smiled.

McKinney was skilled with a knife. In fact, he didn't think his partner had ever lost a knife fight. Sandford didn't move. By the time he got to the fight, McKinney might be cleaning blood off his knife. If so, McKinney could ride down to him. If not... if not, he'd be one on one with Cully. From what he'd been told, going one on one with Cully could be dangerous.

He slowly backed away. If McKinney won the fight, fine. If not...

~***~

Cully's knife slashed thorough the rain and slit his opponent's arm. McKinney clenched his teeth and slashed back, but Cully jumped out of the way. The ground was difficult to move on because of the mud. Cully also kept his gaze toward the bank, in case Sandford showed up. McKinney lunged again, but Cully jumped to the side.

Cully flipped his knife up in his hand. "This is too slow," he said.

He raised the knife and pitched it at McKinney. The knife thudded into his chest, close to his heart. McKinney opened his mouth, but no sound came out. He looked down at the handle then raised his head to look at Cully again. But Cully had already drawn his pistol, turned around, and was looking over the bank. As McKinney fell toward the ground, Cully scrambled over the top and stood up. Due to the dark clouds, vision was poor, but he thought he saw a shadow scramble back behind a tree.

Two shots came from the location of the shadow. Cully dropped back into the gully for cover.

After firing, Sandford jammed his foot into the stirrup and mounted. He spurred his horse. He turned his horse around once and looked backed.

"There'll be another time, Cully. A better time," he said, then headed south.

Cully heard the hoofbeats and looked out. He saw the retreating horse. "Coward," he said. "But I didn't expect anything more from a gunrunner." In the rain, he doubted he could find the outlaw.

"But we'll meet again," he said. "Sooner than you expect."

Chapter 7

He walked over to the dead man. Blood had mixed with the rain and mud to give the earth a crimson stain. He rolled him over. Cully didn't know him. To the best of his knowledge, he had never seen the man before. He grasped the knife and yanked it out of the man's chest, wiping the blood on his pants, then stuck it back in its sheath. He sighed. "Suppose I have to bury you, but danged if I'm going to do it in the rain."

The man's horse stood nearby silently. Cully walked over to it and grabbed the reins. He whistled for Samson, then he and the two horses walked toward the trees. They would provide a degree of cover. When he got to his destination, he took a quick look at Samson's foot. As the rain slackened, he saw the problem. A small sharp pebble had become wedged in his foot. He reached into his pocket and brought out a small jackknife. He flicked open the blade and pried the pebble from the horse's foot then eased the leg back to the ground.

"Shouldn't be bad, Samson, but I needed to get that out. We'll rest you a while, and you'll be fine." He grinned. "I'll have to dig a grave. Well, I don't have to, but I suppose I should. Hate to leave a man for the vultures, even a bad man." He looked around. The rain was almost back to a smattering. "That's one good thing about the rain, I guess. It will make the digging easier. Shouldn't take long at all."

He sat down by a tree and leaned against the trunk. He put his hat over his eyes. A few friends had said he could fall asleep anywhere, anytime. To a great extent, that was true. He had an amazing capacity to fall asleep quickly, no matter what was going on around him. His father had the same trait, one not shared by his mother, to her great exasperation. He remembered any number of nights when she walked the floor of their home, worried about something, while his father was snoring peacefully in bed.

"How do you do that?" she had asked her husband one afternoon, frustration in her tone.

"You're not listening to my sermons my dear," his father had serenely replied. "First Peter, five seven. 'Casting all your care upon him; for he careth for you.' If you cast the cares away, you can sleep better."

His mother never became as good as his father in casting away her cares, but she did get better at it.

As the rain stopped, Cully grinned and closed his eyes.

A short time later, he checked the saddlebags of the dead man's horse but found nothing of value. The horse was a black gelding who seemed friendly enough. Cully gave him a pat. "You appear to be a fine mount. Sorry you got tied up with such a bad fellow," he said.

He walked over to the dead man and dragged him to an isolated area. He checked the man's pockets and found fifty dollars but no identification. Cully pocketed the cash.

"Well, since it won't do you any more good, I may as well take it. You can pay me for your burial. When I get to the next town, I'll have a doctor check this wound. You can pay for that, too, because of all the trouble you caused," he said.

The wound hurt more than he thought it would. A stoic man, he wasn't about to complain. He ignored pain as best he could, but he also knew wounds could fester. It was wise to have a doctor look at them. He looked at the pink, bloody skin over his shoulder. It was ugly enough and painful, but the bullet hadn't hit a vein or bone. *So I'll probably live*, he thought wryly. Although burying the cowboy wasn't going to help it heal. He looked at the dead man.

"It's going to be a shallow grave, cowboy. I'm not giving any extra shovelfuls. In the profession you were in, you're lucky you're getting this courtesy."

After he dug the grave, he found two sticks of wood and made a cross to stick at the grave. He paused and took off his hat.

"Lord, this man was a no-good, back-shootin', vicious outlaw who cared nothing about any person 'cept himself. You may do with him as you will," Cully said. He put his hat back. "And there's one more comin' to you soon."

He looked down the trail as he mounted Samson.

"There's just two of us now," he said to the wind. "Just you and me. Both wounded. Man against man."

~****~

Cully, his shirt off, winced when the doctor wiped the salve on his wound. He didn't like showing pain, but he almost yelled when the orange liquid hit his skin. He stiffened and inhaled. "What is that, doc?" he said.

"It's very effective for wounds. This medicine is difficult to pronounce, but it will help keep you alive," Doctor Tom

Harkin said. Harkin was a young man with brown, wavy hair and a quick smile.

"If it keeps me alive, I guess it's worth the pain. Although I don't think that wound would have killed me."

"Might have. It wasn't too serious, but you shouldn't ignore any wound. It's bandaged now and maybe won't even leave a scar."

"If it does, it won't be the first one I have, and it probably won't be the last, either."

"Maybe you should try another profession."

"In time, doc, but not yet."

Harkin put the bottle back on a shelf. "Anyway, you'll be fine. Hope you catch that man you spoke of. A man giving guns to renegades should be shot... or hanged."

"I think he may have been shot but not in a vital spot, unfortunately. Didn't see any other man with a wound today?"

"No, you're the first gunshot wound I've seen in two months. And the last one was accidental."

"Mine wasn't. I intended to shoot Sandford, and he intended to shoot me," Cully said, smiling. "When I see him again, I plan to shoot him again."

The doctor grinned. "I wish you well."

"By the way, have you been here long? You look young."

"Been here three years. I roam a bit. I'm a traveling doctor. My rounds are three small towns near here. Stay here a few days then move to another town," Harkin said.

"Then you can tell me something. I'm heading to Grants. Any towns between here and there?"

The doctor shook his head. "No towns, but there is a small settlement, goes by the name of Bluewater. Grants is southeast, and there's not much between here and there but flat spaces and jackrabbits. That's one of the towns I travel to, and I've never liked the trip. That's not fun traveling. You still got a little woods to go through, maybe eight to ten miles of it, then hard land. Rocky land. If you're tracking someone, it will be easy for him to give you the slip. You can't pick up tracks when you hit the rocky flats. Not much cover either. You ride about a dozen miles, and then you're near Grants."

"Thank you, doctor. How much do I owe you?"

"Two dollars will do it."

"Not a bad price for keeping me alive."

~****~

Samson was hitched to a post behind the livery stable. The owner patted Samson as Cully approached.

"You have a fine horse here, Mr. Cully. A very fine horse."

Cully nodded. "I always thought so. How's he doing?"

"He'll be fine. But you were right to check on his leg when you noticed the slight limp. And I'm glad you got the pebble out quickly. That could have caused a worse injury if he had run on that leg for long." He shook his head. "At times, I don't think this land is fit for man nor animals."

"I understand the sentiment."

"I put a poultice on and suggest you leave it until morning, just in case. I can keep him here over night if you're staying."

Cully nodded. "Yes, I can let him rest a night. I'm going to catch an outlaw, but I'm not going to lose my horse doing it."

"I gave Samson a checkup since I had him here, and everything looks fine. He's very healthy, not too thin and not too fat, great coordination, moves well, seems to like humans."

"He does. At times I think he likes humans more than I do. And he's probably got more two-legged friends than I do."

The livery owner laughed.

"I'd like to get a good meal before I hit the trail again. What's the best restaurant in town?"

"The best and only restaurant in town is about two blocks from here, just across the street from the sheriff's office. The High Canyon is actually a very good place to eat. Run by Stan and Gladys Trimmer. Both know how to cook well, and they are very friendly people. You'll get a good meal there."

"Thank you. If they're that good, I'll stay tomorrow and have breakfast before I go," Cully said. "And I assume you have a hotel in town too."

"Sure do. One of those, too. And you're in luck. You will be able to get a good night's sleep. I sleep in a room beside the stable but when I can't stand the cot—don't have a bed—I slip over there and get a room."

"Then my night is set. I'll need to pick up some grub tomorrow and be off. Oh, I do need to pick up some bullets too."

"Bullets?"

"Yes. I used some getting here. Have a feeling I'll be using some more before the trip is done."

Chapter 8

The next morning, Cully rolled his gear in his pack and saddled Samson. He checked with the livery owner first and was pleased to hear his horse was fine. He mounted and headed out on the street. The road was to the southeast. He figured he'd pick up Sandford's trail somewhere along the way. Samson trotted cleanly down the road with no trace of a limp in his step.

Cully sang softly as he rode. He had spent a year punching cattle, and even if a cowpuncher couldn't carry a tune, he sang to the animals. Cattle are restless and can be spooked easily. And when they spook, they can stampede. A cattle stampede is one of the worst things you can see on this earth. Five hundred head of cattle running toward you, shaking the ground. The earth literally trembles. If you get caught in front of the charging herd, they'll run you down and trample you. There's hardly enough left to pick up to put in a grave.

But the cows do like songs. Singing, no matter how badly off-key, calms them. So the drovers sing to the ornery cattle until their throats are dry. Cully had sung countless renditions of "Get Along Little Doggie" and countless more of "The Yellow Rose of Texas." The cows never complained, and thankfully, he had never experienced a stampede.

The sun sent long, orange rays across the landscape. A squirrel chirped from a tree he passed and leaped to another branch. An opossum wandered across the road and into a dark section of the forest. He was a late runner. Usually opossums don't come out until dark and don't stay out when the day comes. They are night creatures seeking prey in darkness. Cully grinned. He was seeking prey himself.

He guessed the outlaw would stay on the road to Grants and then maybe keep going to Albuquerque. Or would Sandford want to try facing his tracker? Cully sensed the outlaw would fight when he had to but preferred to stay away from gunplay.

Samson came to a crossroads. Cully looked north and south. A wind blew across the land, which was fine with Cully. A breeze would ease the heat of the day. He halted Samson while he rolled a cigarette. He spied a rider coming from the south.

He looked relaxed in the saddle. He was a short man with a little too much belly but he wore a big smile. His wide blue eyes appeared friendly. As he rode up, he waved hello. "Howdy."

"Good morning," Cully said. "Headed my way?"

"If you're going to Texas, I am."

Cully smiled. "Well, I'm taking the road to Texas, but I'm not going all the way."

"Then I'll ride with you a ways if you don't mind."

"Don't mind at all. My name's Cully."

"I'm Pete Lawrence. Just came back from driving a herd to Mexico. Long journey but got some good money from it."

"Going to spend it in Texas?" Cully said.

Pete shook his head. "Going to get married. Left my engaged in Texas. Going to marry her and let her spend the money." He turned his horse and rode beside Samson as both mounts trotted toward Grants.

"Congratulations."

"Yep. Betty didn't want me to go, but I told her we needed money for the marriage. I didn't want to start off broke. I have a good grubstake now. She lives not far over the border in Tascosas. Wrote her when we got to our destination in Mexico. Told her I'd be coming back with the money. That was four days ago. In a couple of weeks, I'll be knocking on her door."

"Wish you the best."

"Thank you, sir." Pete looked around. "Not many people traveling today. What are you doing out here, Cully?"

"Lookin' for a man."

"Assume there's a reason you're looking for him."

"Up in Colorado, which is my home grounds, he sold guns and whiskey to some Apaches. I'm gonna bring him back to face justice. Either up there or at the end of my gun."

"That's bad business. Hope you get him. The man ran off to New Mexico?"

Cully nodded. "He was in Gallup, but he knew I was sniffing out his trail, so he's moving on."

"He keeps moving south, you may not have to worry about him."

Cully looked over at him. "What do you mean by that?"

"I'm just back from Mexico. Word is Red Fox, a Comanche, has also come up and brought a bunch of warriors with him. It's said some renegades are planning to join up with him. When they do, this part of the state may be turned into a cemetery. That's why I'm heading east when we hit Albuquerque. That trail takes me away from trouble not toward it. That's a little out of my way, but I can circle around and get back on a trail to Texas without worrying about Red Fox and his band. Hear they're after blood, and I don't plan to give them any of mine."

"Thanks for telling me, Pete."

"If your wanted man heads south, the Comanches may finish your job for you. That would be somewhat ironic. A man who sells guns to Indians gets killed by them," Pete said.

Cully nodded. "That's right. Some might not find that humorous but I'd laugh at it. It would be a just end for Sandford."

"That his name? Sandford."

"Yep. It's nice to know and it's always good to get the right name on the tombstone." Cully's eyes continually scanned the ground. His lips jerked when he saw the cigar butt. It had been tossed to the side of the road. He halted Samson and stepped down.

Pete also stopped his mount when Cully walked over to the cigar and picked it up. "Mean something?" Pete said.

"The man I'm tracking smokes a cigar. Guess I must be on the right track. Only seen signs of two people this morning. You and him."

"Then it does narrow down the suspects."

Cully studied the burnt tobacco. He guessed the cigar had been dropped several hours before, which meant Sandford didn't have too much of a lead on him. After the gun battle yesterday, he may have found a secure location and slept late.

Cully's wound was slight but didn't bother him. He wondered if Sandford's was more serious. Perhaps serious enough to slow him down a bit. He put his hand on his saddle horn.

"You know this country?" he asked Pete.

"Not an expert but I've been through here a few times."

"What's between here and Grants?"

He shook his head. "Not much. And Grants isn't that much a town. After that, there's rugged, rocky terrain then a desert. This is land that's not hospitable to people. Only Comanches could live on much of it. As it is, I don't see how the people in Grants stick with it."

Cully grinned. "Indians have been here for hundreds of years, if not more."

"We ain't Indians."

"True enough."

A brown hawk flew gracefully overhead, pivoting as he lowered and winged over their heads.

"Wish I could soar," Cully said. "Could spot Sandford easily then."

"If he keeps heading this direction, he may not be hard to find. Only one road past Grants, and it heads to Albuquerque then on to Texas."

Cully lifted himself onto Samson's back. "I haven't been to Texas in a while. Maybe I'll be roaming down there."

Pete grunted. "Some places in Texas are nice. A lot of other places I wouldn't spit at."

They spurred their horses, and the sun rose in the sky. A pale yellow orb eased up in the sky. The two felt the heat in the air. They would be sweating soon.

"So when's the wedding?" Cully asked.

"Two days after I arrive. Gives Betty one day to pick out the wedding dress, if she hasn't already. We'll head off to the preacher's and say the words. Then there are no more long trail drives. Got a job lined up in town."

"Really? That will make the wife happy."

"It sure will. Got a friend who has a small spread near town. He needs some help, so I'm going to give him some. He'll pay well, and I know he won't cheat me. It will be enough for Betty and me to live on, til I find something different. She wants a family, so we're gonna have children, that's for sure."

"Since I was a child once, I think that's a good idea," Cully said.

Pete laughed. "Betty wants a big family, at least five or six kids."

"Better have a big house."

Chapter 9

From his perch on the huge oak that he had climbed, Night Hawk stared with hatred at the two white men. Night Hawk was the name his fellow Comanches had given him. He killed during the day, too, but he excelled at night fighting. He could move with the speed of a mountain lion and was just as deadly. One quick thrust of his knife had brought death to many men. Now he and Red Fox would deliver even more death on their enemies. Perhaps the two white men riding toward him would be among those slain by him and his fellow warriors.

He felt a strong desire to sneak up on the two and stab their hearts, but he held back. Red Fox wanted no violence and no deaths until the attack that would take the white man by surprise. The town of Grants might be the target. It was a small town. When all the warriors joined Red Fox, there would be fifty in his band. A swift attack might leave the town in flames and dozens of white men dead.

The two men rode slowly. With a swift leap, he jumped to another tree. He saw no reason to follow the two. If they kept traveling, they might be fortunate and miss the attack. They might be past Grants when Red Fox yelled the war cry. The whites had taken their land, the land their ancestors had walked and rode on for hundreds of years. Now the whites must pay.

He turned toward the west and saw no others on the road or in the forest. No soldiers. No bands of armed men. This was a good time to strike. He would soon wear the scalps of his enemies on his belt. All of Red Fox's band would know how many whites he had killed. It would bring him great honor among the warriors.

Glancing around one last time, he began to descend. He eased down the tree and jumped to the ground. His horse was nearby. He took another look toward the two men. He would abide by Red Fox's words. Nothing must interfere with the planned attack. When the news of it spread throughout the territory, other Comanches would join the band, and with their help, there would be other, even bigger victories. All of his brothers must join together soon to defeat the white man. The white encroachment must be stopped now or it would be too late. If they waited, the white tide would never recede and their ancestral land would be gone forever.

He jumped on his mount's back and rode slowly and cautiously through the forest. He did not want to be seen, not yet. Soon the whites would see him and all his brothers in war-paint, yelling for blood. But not yet. As for now, he must move like the wind, silently and unseen.

But soon Night Hawk would spread bloodshed and death.

~***~

"So you were in the war?" Cully asked his companion.

Pete nodded. "Joined in '64 when I was old enough to. Turned eighteen and signed up after the family had a birthday party. I'm from Illinois, and I lived near the hometown of President Lincoln. We were very big on Honest

Abe. Never did meet him, but I was in town when he rode by one day going to a political event. We were big Union people too. No one liked slavery in my hometown."

"I understand why. My father was a minister, and he detested slavery. He preached against it and lost some members of his congregation. Told them it was evil and we should oppose it with all the strength we have. So where did you serve?"

"I was with Sherman when he plowed through Georgia. He wiggled his way around north Georgia and finally found a way to head for Atlanta. We whipped the rebs, and after that, there wasn't much left of their army. Then we marched to Savannah and took the city without much resistance. You hear about the telegram General Sherman sent Mister Lincoln?"

"Can't say I did."

"We took Savannah in December, although I don't remember which day. So Sherman, he whipped up a telegram stating, 'Mr. President, I present you the city of Savannah as a Christmas present.' I'm sure the president smiled when he got the telegram."

Cully chuckled. "I'm sure he did too."

"Then we marched up South Carolina and tore up the place. We considered South Carolina not much better than hell. That was where the war started, when the rebs fired on Fort Sumter. I wasn't there at the beginning of the war, but I was there at the end. When Confederate General Johnson surrendered to Sherman in North Carolina. Wasn't much left of the rebel army by that time. Then we all went home. After I went home, I went west and wound up in Texas."

"Did the folks in Texas mind you had fought for the Union?"

"Not really. Texas had basically been out of the war for about two years, ever since we gained control of the Mississippi, so all the raw feelings had settled down. Didn't have much trouble. Sort of rambled until I met Betty. Then I wanted to settle down. You say you are from Colorado?"

"Yes."

"Magnificent state. All those mountains. You don't see such beautiful scenery back east. I've been to the Continental Divide. You can hardly imagine such a thing, and suddenly there it is, right before you. It gives you a sense of... smallness yet a sense of awe too."

Cully nodded. "That's true. My father always loved going to look at it. Said it gave you a sense of the divine." He paused for a moment. "And yep, it did."

"Yes, once you see that you never forget it."

As they rounded a curve, a stage station came into sight. There was a ranch house with a corral with four horses roaming around. A barn was across from the house. Two men stood in the yard.

"A depot," said Cully.

"Yes, the stagecoach line has one here. They need to water their horses or, at times, get fresh ones. I had almost forgotten about this. They might have grub they can offer us. It's been a while since I've passed by, but if I remember, they're very friendly."

One of the men waved as they approached. He was a tall man with blond hair and a fair complexion, although Cully didn't see how a man could stay pale in the New Mexico sun.

"Hello, care to step down and sit a spell?"

"I wouldn't mind a brief rest," Cully said.

"Then climb down. We keep food ready in the house, if you would like something. Water your horses too." He pointed where three oaks grew together. "That water trough is in the shade, and it keeps the water cool. Your horses will enjoy it." He smiled and almost laughed. "We don't get many visitors, but we like those we do get."

Cully and Pete climbed down from their horses.

The other man was younger than the first but had a quick smile and a deep voice. "That's true. Usually we get only stages on this road. Today we've had one other man who rode through. He wasn't very friendly though."

Cully raised his eyebrows. "Another man came this way?"

"Yep, about two hours ago. Just rode in and asked if he could water his horse. We said sure. Tried to talk to him, but he said nothing and looked like he didn't want to be bothered. Just watered his horse, got back on, and said thanks as he rode out."

Cully fished in his pocket for the wanted poster. When he found it, he pulled it out and opened it, showing it to the man. "Did he look anything like this?"

The man nodded. "He sure did. That was him." He grabbed the poster and shook his head. "Sorry we didn't know he was wanted. We would have held him for you."

Cully liked the sound and look of the man. He thought the two would have kept Sandford as a prisoner if they had known of his background. The two didn't look menacing, but they had a solidness and an honesty about them. "He head toward Grants?"

"Sure did. Didn't tell us where he's going, but he was heading that way."

"Good."

"I don't see no badge. You're a bounty hunter?"

"At times. I don't mind picking up money, but with this man, I'd hunt him down for free."

Cully walked Samson to the water trough and watched him drink. He tied him under the shade of the trees then walked toward the house.

The blond man offered his hand. "By the way I'm Shep Williams. My partner is Everett Thomas."

"Good to meet ya," Cully said.

~****~

Sandford drained the whiskey bottle of the little liquor left in it. He pulled it from his mouth and looked at it with disgust. *I should have bought two bottles,* he thought, tossing the empty one away. He cursed and shifted in the saddle. The forest was coming to a close, and he was within a few miles of rocky land, barren flats that stretched for at least ten miles. He put his hand on his gun. He had a decision to make. He took off his hat and wiped the sweat off his brow. His back ached where Cully's bullet had caught him.

He wanted to ignore the question poking his brain the way a thorn, caught in your shirt, will poke your skin. He could simply make a flat-out run for Texas, or he could try to lay a trap for Cully and ambush him. The last time, an ambush didn't work out too well, and this time he wouldn't have a friend to help. He'd be on his own. He preferred the first choice. Catch the train in Albuquerque bound for Texas. *Don't stop until I get there.*

An edginess came over him. A feeling deep in his stomach that perhaps he wasn't as good one on one as he thought. He realized, most times in his life when he traded gunfire with opponents, he had been part of a crowd. Almost every time he had been with his gang. He tried to think of a time when he squared off one to one, and he couldn't. Now, even the thought of staring Cully down with no help made his hands sweat. Which is why he needed another bottle. The bottle brings courage, and right now he could use just a little extra.

Cully was tenacious. He probably would not give up. Like a hound after a raccoon, Cully would be on his trail until perdition came. He nodded. He would try another ambush. He might be able to kill Cully on the trail. If he didn't succeed, then he could run for Texas and head straight through to Louisiana. He had always wanted to see Louisiana. He heard New Orleans was a fantastic city. Cully couldn't track him after he boarded the train to Texas. Not even Cully was that good.

He should get behind one of those huge elms and wait for Cully to come up the road. Possibly wait until he rode by, then grab the rifle, aim and fire. Leave the bounty hunter with three or more bullets in his back. Give some buzzards their dinner.

If he did that, he'd have to be very careful. Head off the road and tie his horse so far from the path that Cully couldn't hear any random neighs. Have the rifle ready. If Cully suspected an ambush...he had already had a gunfight with the man and didn't like the result.

He sighed again as he saw the rider coming toward him. He took off his hat and wiped his face again as he watched the rider come closer. The man looked like an ordinary cowhand. He saw an item in the man's saddlebag and smiled. "Howdy," he said.

"Afternoon," the man said as he rode by.

When the rider was about five feet away, Sandford pulled his pistol. This is the way I like it, he thought. No risk, in the back. He aimed and fired twice. Two red holes appeared in the man's shirt. His grip on the reins loosened, and he toppled to the ground. His horse stood still over its rider. Sandford climbed down and walked over to the horse. He flipped open the saddlebag and grabbed the bottle. He had noticed the liquor as the man rode by. He held up the whiskey and laughed.

"Sometimes liquor can be as valuable as gold. I needed a drink." He slapped the bottle with his hand then pulled out the cork and took a long swallow. *Courage when I needed it*, Sandford thought. I can take Cully now.

He would have to find a safe spot until Cully, like the now dead rider, passed on by.

Knowing Cully was behind him was like feeling a hairy tarantula crawling up his back. You had to get rid of it without it killing you. Thinking about it gave you the willies.

He started walking back toward his horse then stopped. He didn't want a body on the path. He groaned and stuck the bottle in his saddle bag. He walked back toward the body, lifted it, and dragged it off the road into the forest. Grunting with the effort, he dragged it five feet from the road then dropped it. He shrugged and went through the man's pockets. He found twenty dollars in his pants but nothing else.

"Well, it'll pay for drinks and dinner in the next town," he said, pocketing the bills.

He looked off and wondered if anyone could see the body from the road. He didn't want anything making Cully suspicious when he came by. Not satisfied, he bent and picked up the body again and dragged it deeper into the forest. When he dropped the body a second time, he noticed markings on the ground.

They worried him.

He eased over and bent down so he could see them better. He had heard rumors of possible renegade Comanches, but he paid them no mind. As he looked at the markings again, he knew he'd made a mistake.

On the ground were signs of unshod horses, the kind Comanches ride. He guessed at least two had come through the area. That was troubling. He wasn't on any reservation land. There shouldn't have been any unshod horses in this area. He looked around quickly, as if a Comanche might jump out from behind a bush. Except for the dead stranger, he hadn't seen any other riders. But some were in the area or had been in the area. He snorted. *Indians are almost as bad as Cully.* He dealt with them in Colorado, but he had no more guns or whiskey. To these Comanches, in New Mexico, he was just another white man to be killed. Still, there couldn't be a large party in the area. If so, he would have seen some sign of them earlier. Perhaps two scouts were sent ahead. If so, the main band of Comanches would be a ways behind.

He ran back to his horse and mounted.

Chapter 10

Shep dished hot stew into a bowl that Cully brought to the stove. Large pieces of beef wedged in with equally large potatoes and a full carrot with rich, brown gravy. Cully's mouth watered as he walked to a table where Pete already sat and was forking a beef slice.

"Great stew. You can cook. It's rare I ever get to eat this good on the trail. Usually it's just campfire cooking," Pete said.

"We try to keep dinner ready for the stagecoach passengers. You never know how long they've been on the road and how hungry they are," Shep said.

Cully forked both meat and potatoes and swallowed the mixture. He smiled. "Wish I could cook like you. I've had too many days and nights when I had to eat my own grub, and I wouldn't advise anybody to eat my cooking, man or beast."

"Sorry that other traveler didn't stay around. If he had known you cook this well, he might have stayed for dinner."

"I think Sandford had other things on his mind," Cully said.

"Yeah, probably so," Pete said. "He has to eat on the run. Probably not good for the digestion."

"You two are welcome to stay awhile," Shep said.

Cully shook his head. "Not me. I want to find Sandford as soon as possible. He has a noose waiting for him in Colorado, and I want to see he gets to the cemetery on time."

Shep brought two cups of coffee and set them down before Cully and Pete.

Cully swallowed another bite of the stew then sipped the coffee. "You said Sandford kept going southeast when he rode out?"

"Sure did. He didn't seem real nervous but didn't appear like he wanted to stick around neither. Still, I didn't think he was a man on the run."

"Would you have a map in the station?" Cully asked.

"Sure do. A good-sized one. It's in the next room. When you get through eating, I'll show it to you."

"What's after Grants?"

"You get a little way outside of the town, and you hit a desert. About twenty miles of it. Darn hot one too. I've had to cross that twice. If you can get through in a day, you better know where the water holes are, unless you know how to get water from cactus. And if you do, you better give it to your horse first. You don't want your horse to die on you out there. If he does, just pull your gun and point it to your head. That would be better than dying of thirst."

Cully nodded. He had spent a little time in deserts. It reminded him of one of the few sermons his father preached that he disagreed with. "There are times with suffering can teach men and women valuable lessons," the pastor told his congregation once. "After you come out of a crisis, you find it has made you stronger and better able to deal with the next one."

Cully had pondered that sermon for a while, but he still didn't agree with it. Once he had a tough time in a desert. Pursued by some Arapaho warriors, he had run out of water and traded bullets with them. He killed two and wounded several others, but he was a long way from civilization and out of water. He and his horse just barely made it. When they reached the water hole, he literally dived into it, and his horse must have drunk for fifteen minutes. The only thing suffering taught him was he didn't want any more of it. However, it did give him a great appreciation for the small things in life—such as a drink of water. Never a man to complain, he discovered he griped even less after nearly dying in the stinking desert. If he was having a bad day, he would go get a drink of water and smile. However bad the day was, it wasn't as bad as the thirstiest day in his life.

He gave a rueful grin. Suffering might not have taught him much, but it did remind him to keep out of deserts. He scooped up the last bit of meat and a small potato and washed it down with coffee. "What do I owe you?" he said.

"Not a thing. We cook for the passengers at no charge."

"But I'm not a passenger."

"We would have cooked, anyway. No charging you. But if you're through, come on and I'll show you the map."

As Cully stood up, someone banged on the door and then burst in. Using gloves, he slapped dust from clothes.

"Jim, what are you doing here?" Shep said. "Gentlemen, this is Jim Langer, one of Wells Fargo's men. A troubleshooter and all-around good guy. Sit down and have some dinner, Jim."

The man shook his head. He was middle aged with blond hair falling over his eyes. He wiped it back with his hand. He looked weary, as if he had been riding a long time. "But I will have some water," he said. He walked to a water bucket, lifted the cup to his lips and drank all the water.

"What's got you so riled up, Jim?" Shep said.

"A Comanche called Red Fox. There's been rumors he just came out of Mexico with three dozen or more warriors. I've been checking it out. And it's true. From what I can tell, they're heading this way. You better abandon the station for a while and get into Grants. You're a sitting target here."

Shep shook his head. "I'm not running. We've had Indian raids before. In case you've forgotten, Mr. Thomas and I are good shots. The last raid on this station was three years ago, and if you remember, we left three men dead and had a couple more wounded. Our aim hasn't slipped any since then."

Langer raised the cup again but ducked toward the bucket and poured the cup of water over his head. Water flowed down his face. When he shook his head, water drops spurted all over the room. He sighed and planted his hat back on his wet hair. "You don't understand. That was different. Back three years ago, you were facing a dozen, maybe less. A dozen. Three dozen will be different. Fifty would be even worse. You can't take on fifty men."

"Well, fifty Comanches wouldn't have a big problem taking out two of us. Besides, why would they hit us?"

"You have horses here, prime targets."

"Where are these Comanches?" Shep said.

"I'm not sure, somewhere east of the Arizona border. I'm sure they sent out scouts and lookouts. And I'm sure many random warriors throughout the whole state are riding to join up with them."

"Sit down and have some grub, Jim."

Langer started to shake his head but stopped. "You know... I am hungry. Maybe I could use some grub. So could my horse. He needs water, too."

"Then I suggest you feed and water him and sit down for some grub." He gestured to Cully and Pete. "Those two gentlemen will tell you it's very good."

"That we can do," Cully said.

"If you got a long ride ahead of you, then you'll need strength. Or you can stay here if you like."

Langer nodded. "Let me go take care of my horse. Then I'll have a plate of stew and see."

"Sounds good," Shep said.

Cully walked into the next room and saw a huge wall map showing this part of the territory. The way station was marked in red with the road running before it. The forest continued for about ten miles and then the road entered Grants. The desert did take over the road just a few miles past the town. Routine country seemed to take over after the desert ended. But in New Mexico, routine country meant rough country and rough riding.

"It's not really scenic. Been to Colorado. You have some beautiful country up there. But this is not Colorado. It's New Mexico. It's fit for Gila monsters and rattlesnakes, and that's about it."

Cully nodded. The trail definitely didn't look pleasant. "Thank you," he said. "Reckon I'll be on my way."

"Wish you the best," Shep said.

~***~

He needed a partner, Sandford thought. An ambush was easier with two people. Getting a man in a crossfire is a sure way to kill him. But for a crossfire to be effective, you have to have a second man. Looking back on the trail, Sandford thought he had found the best place to surprise Cully. When the trail was less than a mile away from Grants, it took a sharp turn. Cully would turn his horse left to go around the curve and then hit a straight line toward the town. A large curve but when it straightened out any sniper would have a clear shot at him. The sides of the road were hilly. A sniper could hide behind a tree and get a perfect bead on a rider coming around the curve. There wasn't a better place for an ambush, Sandford decided.

He would have to wait for his target. He didn't know how long it would take Cully to catch up with him, so he would have to be patient. But if he was fortunate, Cully would be dead before the day was done.

He rode up the incline to the trees to look for a spot. It took him several minutes to decide on the back of a tall oak. It was an outlier. Four or five trees were between it and the road, but they didn't block his vision. A horse would be walking into his line of sight. He patted the bark of the tree. This was the best he could do. The shot shouldn't be too difficult.

He had missed Cully the first time. He couldn't make another mistake. You can't give a skilled hunter a second chance. If you do, they dump you in the ground and say a few words over you. He looked around, as if searching for another that might improve his chances of killing Cully. But he saw nothing but trees and swaying branches. This would have to do. One last chance.

He had time for a fire. He'd have an early dinner. Didn't want to get hungry while he was waiting. *Start a small campfire now. Indians can't see smoke at night, but they can smell it. So they know some white man is in the darkness.* He doubted Cully could smell smoke, but he wouldn't put it past him, and he couldn't take any chances. He'd cook a meal now and bury the campfire after he was through. Then there would just be silence and no smoke when Cully came along.

Lousy luck, he decided. It was just lousy luck Cully had picked one of his wanted posters or somehow sniffed his tail. But now he would have to deal with it.

But it was a bit ominous. Sometimes if a bit of bad luck hit you, another spot of bad luck would find you. It accumulated. Would there be more bad luck finding him? He shook his head to clear his mind. *Forget about luck, good or bad*, he told himself. *Just focus on one thing.*

Killing Cully.

Chapter 11

Cully and Pete climbed onto their respective horses, tipped their hats to the two men, and headed out toward Grants.

"Come back anytime," Shep shouted. "It's always nice to have company."

"That's the best meal I ever had out on the road," Pete told Cully.

"Sure was. I always hated eating my own cooking. Glad I didn't have to today," Cully said.

They spurred their horses down the trail. The evening sky slowly dissolved into a gray mist as the sun lowered and clouds congregated. A slight wind blew in from the south. The other sound was the steady clomping of the hooves of the two horses.

"What do you think about that talk of Comanches?" Pete said.

Cully shrugged. "This is the West. We hear those stories from time to time. I'm not dismissing them. Any man would be a fool to do so. But if a Comanche war party has crossed the border, like you mentioned earlier, I figure the cavalry knows about it and is dealing with it."

"Yes, but it makes me nervous knowing some Comanches are nearby."

"They're hard fighters and hard men. We beat them because we have more men and better weapons, not because we have more guts. I respect them as opponents. Was always told, too, if a Comanche gives you his word, he's good for it. Known a few white men are good like that, but only a few," Cully said.

"The problem is not that a Comanche or two will keep his word. The problem is what they say. When he says he'll kill you and take your hair, then you can be assured he's running toward you with his knife out."

Cully smiled. "There may be some truth in that too." He chuckled as he looked down the trail. "I would personally like to shoot Sandford, but I wouldn't mind if he fell into the hands of Comanches. That would be a fitting end for a man who traded guns to Indians."

"Alas, there is not always justice, at least not in this world."

"But there is in the next, or at least that's what my father believed. He told his congregation there will be a Judgment Day for all men. You will stand and give an account of yourself before the Supreme Judge."

"I agree with that," Pete said. "I'm a Christian. I admit the reason—the initial reason I became a Christian—was not admirable, but I am a believer now. I believe there's a God in heaven and that Jesus, my Savior, will return to Earth."

Cully looked over at his riding partner. It was not unusual to find a Christian on the trail. His father was not the only preacher in the West. There were many roving ministers in these lands. The West was considered fertile missionary ground for many denominations. "I'm curious. What was your initial reason for getting converted?"

"Because Betty refused to be courted by anyone but a believer. If you were a pagan, she had nothing to do with you. Wouldn't give you the time of day. Since she was the prettiest thing I'd ever seen, I figured a woman like that was worth a conversion."

Cully's laughter roared between the trees and shook a few leaves off branches. He grabbed his canteen and sipped some water but laughed so much drops fell onto his shirt and neck. "My father, in addition to being a preacher, enjoyed history. We always had history books around the house. Back in the Middle Ages, the Protestants and Catholics were fighting over in Europe. I think it was a King Henry who was offered France, and particularly, Paris, if he would convert to Catholicism. He agreed. When later asked about it, he said, 'Paris is worth a mass.' No doubt he was right, and I'm sure you were right too, Pete. I'm sure Betty was worth a conversion."

"But I do have to give up liquor. Betty won't let any in the house."

Cully nodded. "Probably wise. Probably be good for you. My mother didn't want any liquor in our house either, but neither did my father. That was one of the many things they agreed on."

"Have any family, Cully? Have two brothers myself."

"Have a younger sister. She's married and lives on a place near Durango." He sighed. "That's why I hunt men. Or one reason I hunt men. Outlaws killed my parents, and I want to rid the earth of them. But I have a nice little spread near

Durango. I'm putting money into it and getting it ready to move there permanent if I ever stop hunting men."

"Gonna run cattle?"

Cully shook his head. "Gonna be a horse ranch. I like horses, and they have an affinity for me. Someday I'd like to study veterinary medicine so I'd know what to do when a horse gets sick."

Pete let out a deep laugh. It was more of a belly rumble. When Cully heard it, he laughed to.

Cully stiffened and jerked the reins to the left.

"Something wrong?"

"Thought I saw something. A shadow there between the trees. A shadow where one shouldn't be."

Pete stopped his horse and looked where Cully pointed. "Don't see anything," he said. "Looks clear."

Cully waited a moment then nodded. "Guess so. Sometimes a shadow is just a shadow." He waited another thirty seconds then spurred Samson on.

"I wouldn't want your job, Cully. Seems to me you have to look over your shoulder most of your life."

"You get used to it." Cully rode a few paces. "To fight it out," he sang. "On this here line…"

Pete joined in. "O, General Grant's the man…"

Cully traveled some trails where he needed to be silent. This wasn't one of them. There was no reason for silence now. Let the birds chime in for that matter.

"To reconstruct this mighty land."

"How many songs you know, Cully?" said Pete.

"Only about twenty, but I know them real well," said Cully. "Those twenty are road songs, songs the cattle enjoy.

Know about twenty hymns, too. We sang in church every Sunday." He laughed. "However, believe it or not, the beeves often took a hankering to 'Amazing Grace.'"

"Is that a fact?"

"That's a fact. They mooed along to it. Cattle appreciated singing, Even off-key singing." Cully said.

"You know, I was out with three other drovers one night, and I never heard such caterwauling. Think we all were singing different songs, and none of us could carry a tune. That was awful. I mean that was pure agony for the ears, but the beeves seemed to like it. They walked around chewing grass contentedly."

"Well, there's no accounting for musical tastes," Cully said. "My father told me in the early days of his ministry, he would walk out in the fields and preach to the cows. He said they seemed to like his sermons. Maybe they like singing and preaching."

"Probably would have liked it better if he sang his sermons to them."

While talking, Cully kept his gaze to the ground. He paused his horse when the first clear image of a hoof print appeared. The ground was hard and would get harder, but the horse had stepped in a soft patch of ground. Most of the hoof mark could be seen. He nodded. A rider, most likely Sandford, had come this way. Another mile down the trail, he saw another sign. Something had stepped on the sagebrush, which was now mashed down. Another sign of a rider.

Cully wondered if the man would stop in Grants. Did he want some grub or water? He didn't stop at the way station.

Would he risk that? No, probably not. If there was a sheriff in the town, Sandford would need to keep low. He wouldn't want a sheriff and a bounty hunter after him. No doubt he would avoid the town. So would he go around it? Only way. Cully thought perhaps he should speed up and try to kill Sandford before he got to the rocky land flats. It was clear the rider who trampled the sage was not traveling fast. Cully might catch him and bring the chase to a conclusion. He spurred Samson to move quicker.

Pete started singing another Western ballad.

Cully's eyes darted back and forth. Few things in the forest escaped his gaze. "Let's move a little faster," he said.

"That's OK with me. Hope we get some wind. No matter what time of day, this region is hot." Pete switched to another tune. Although in New Mexico, he sang about the Yellow Rose of Texas.

But like a rope locked on a runaway steer, Cully's mind focused on another matter. Sandford had tried one ambush. What were the chances he'd try another? He shifted in the saddle. If Sandford was going to try something, this would be the time. Before he got to the town. Sandford would have to pick his time and place. But he was running out of space. Grants wasn't far away. The thought didn't bother Cully. He didn't mind tracking a suspect down, but neither would he object when the wanted man decided to save him some trouble with a one-on-one confrontation. He looked around.

This might be the place.

He placed his hand on his gun as he straightened in the saddle. He saw nothing to alarm him. And sensed nothing dangerous in the trees. At least not here. But he would be watching.

Pete had returned to a version of "General Grant's the Man." He didn't have a bad voice. Maybe it had improved by singing to the cattle every day on the drive down to Mexico. But considering Sandford might be up ahead, Cully turned and started to tell him to ride silently. Then he stopped. He grinned. Perhaps Pete's singing might have some benefit. The more he thought about it, the more the singing sounded very good to him.

"Pete, you know this trail?" Cully asked.

"Yep, not too well though. I've only traveled it a couple of times."

"Know what's ahead of us. Any surprises?"

"There are no surprises in this country. Just more desert and more sand and more rocks and more creepy little four-footed toads."

Cully pointed toward the trail. "I mean the road. Any changes?"

"Not many. Basically straight. There is one wide curve about two miles ahead. Get a pretty big swing."

"Is that right?" Cully said.

"Yep, then it's just a straight shot to Grants. When you leave Grants, there's not much on the other side of the town except a desert and Gila monsters..."

Chapter 12

Sandford walked his horse about twenty yards from his firing position and tied him to a tree. Then he walked back and squatted down behind the tree that had a clear sight of the road as it curved. He had walked out to the road and saw that a rider would have difficulty seeing him in the forest, but he could see a rider clearly. If he missed or only wounded Cully, the man didn't have much cover. He would have to scamper about twenty yards to find a tree large enough to hide him. And if by some miracle he made it without being shot again, Sandford thought all he had to do was put three or four bullets in Cully's horse. That would stop the bounty hunter. It was still a couple of miles to town, and Cully would have a long walk, especially carrying a saddle. By the time he made it to Grants and got a horse, Sandford knew he'd be halfway to Albuquerque. He'd be riding day and night to put space between him and the bounty hunter. But this should work, he told himself. Cully should be dead before he had a chance to reach for his gun.

He leaned against the tree, a rifle in his hand. Here he was back to waiting. He pulled a cigar from his pocket and lit it. Not many things you can do while waiting. Smoking was one of them. He hoped Cully didn't take too long. He got edgy when he waited, and when nervous, a man can make mistakes. He eased his rifle up and aimed at the spot a man would be when riding down the road. He checked his shirt pocket. He had three cigars. Probably smoke them all before getting a shot at Cully.

He had smoked only one and tossed it into the forest when he heard singing. The off-key song alerted him. He tensed and gripped his rifle more tightly. He peered toward the road, but as yet, no riders were heading his way. But the song continued. A man was singing "Oh! Susanna" Or trying to sing it. The singer was off key. Would that be Cully? He thought, *Why not?* The bounty man wasn't expecting an ambush. No reason why he shouldn't sing. Sandford raised the rifle to his shoulder. Whoever it was should be making the turn shortly.

He first saw the head of the horse, then the horse and rider came into view. The man kept singing. He'd die with a song on his lips, Sandford thought. The rider was not yet in range. But in a minute or two... His hands began to sweat. He wiped them on his pants. He breathed shallowly. In a few seconds, he'd finally be free of Cully. His heart thumped with anticipation. Sandford was not one to hold his emotions in check. The rider came closer. Hooves of his horse clumped on the ground. Thirty seconds...

Sandford blinked. And cursed. Something was wrong. He had gotten a good look at Cully at the gully. The singing man on the horse wasn't the bounty hunter. Cully was taller than this man. The man in the saddle was shorter. Plus the rider carried extra pounds round his belly. Cully was tall and straight. There wasn't an ounce of fat on him. Sandford cursed again. What was the singing man doing here? He raised his rifle. He should kill the man for the aggravation.

"Drop the rifle or die! It's your choice!"

The hard-bitten voice came from behind Sandford. But he didn't dare turn around. Not with the rifle in his hand. He let it drop.

"Very good. Now turn around."

Sandford, with his hands up, turned toward the voice. It was the tall bounty hunter, holding a rifle on him.

"You must be Sandford," Cully said.

"I am. And you're Cully."

"Yep. I'm taking you back to Colorado. You're gonna stand trial, and you're gonna hang. And I'm going to make sure I'm there to see it. I usually don't like hangings much, so don't like watching them, but in your case, I'll make an exception."

"We ain't there yet."

"No, but we will be. But if you try to escape, I'll save the state the trouble of walking you up to the gallows. I'll bury you here and save the taxpayers some money. Never liked burdening the taxpayers." Cully took a step back and waved to Pete. "Got him!"

As Pete waved back, the arrow zoomed toward him and sank into his shoulder. He yelled and plunged forward, causing his horse to jump. The move pushed him down so the next two arrows flowed over him.

At the same time, an arrow thunked into the tree next to Sandford. A bullet from the forest didn't quite miss Cully's leg. He groaned and spun around, falling to the ground. Sandford grabbed his rifle and fired at the two Comanches he spotted advancing toward him. Cully rolled on the incline and came up limping. When he got to his feet, he raced toward the road to help his friend. He zig-zagged through the forest, ignoring the pain in his leg.

Pete had stumbled off his horse, grabbing his rifle and jumping behind a tree. The arrow remained in his shoulder, but he couldn't do anything about it yet. The wound sent jolts of pain through his arm, but he still gripped the rifle tight. He looked around but didn't see any Comanches. He looked behind him. That was where the arrow had come from.

A warrior on the other side of the road jumped up and ran across toward the other side. Pete's bullet caught him mid-stride. When his foot hit the ground, the leg weakened and couldn't hold him. He fell hard on the ground. He gritted his teeth and tried with all his strength to pull himself up. But all his strength was gone. He died on the road.

"Take that!" Pete said. But he knew it had been a lucky shot. With the pain, he found it difficult to keep his arm steady. He groaned again and eased back against the tree.

Cully broke from the trees on the other side of the road and made it across the road, even with his wound. He ran toward Pete.

The man grinned. "Your plan worked."

"Your singing kept his attention while I got behind him. I thought this might be a good place for an ambush," Cully said. "He thought he had me. Sorry for all the trouble, Pete. Didn't mean to get you shot."

Pete shook his head. "Shot with an arrow ain't nothing. We simply pull it out, when we get a chance, that is."

Cully looked at the wound. It could have been worse. The arrowhead hadn't gone in too deep. He should be able to remove it without too much trouble. They heard a gunshot from across the road. Two gunshots.

"Hope that's the Comanches killing Sandford instead of the other way around," Cully said. He reached over, grabbed the arrow and broke it. "Pete, I'll get the arrowhead out just as soon as I'm sure there are no more people around who want to kill us."

"No hurry. It's not going anywhere. Hear anything?"

Cully shook his head. "The Comanches strike fast and quick. Sometimes they leave just as fast... just so long as they don't come back. Stinking bad time. I had Sandford cornered. Now he's got away again."

"You can always give him up and let someone else kill him." Pete groaned with each breath. Cully knew he was in pain. "People like Sandford usually end up dead. If you quit, then some Texas sheriff will shoot him."

"Lot of truth in that," Cully said, still scanning the forest for a shadow that shouldn't be there. "But I would like to be the man who puts a bullet in him, if he isn't hanged."

In the distance, he heard horses' hooves. He turned and saw a rider galloping down the path. It was Sandford.

Cully slapped his rifle. "I wouldn't mind if he were dead. Now I will have to keep tracking him."

Pete had sat down by a tree. "Sorry he's alive."

"He is," Cully said, "but not for too much longer." He sat his rifle down and pulled out his knife. He walked over to Pete. "This is going to hurt some, but I'm pretty good as a cowboy doctor. Grit your teeth. I'm going to have to dig it out. The good news is the wound isn't too deep. The bad news is it's still going to hurt."

"Kinda figured it would."

Cully dug the edge of his knife into Pete's shoulder. He stuck the blade under the arrowhead and flicked it up then grabbed the arrowhead as it emerged from the skin. Pete yelled.

Cully showed the bloody arrowhead to his friend. "Would you like a souvenir?"

"No, I'm not sentimental about getting wounded by Comanches. Just throw it away."

Cully chuckled and tossed the arrowhead into the forest. Then he bandaged up the wound as tight as he could. "Even though that's out, I think we should get to Grants as quick as possible. There may be a doctor there, and he can take a look at my work and check the wound," Cully said.

"I don't think any doctor could have done a better job than you did."

"Even so, if you feel like riding, we should head out."

Pete nodded. "Just give me a minute. And, if you would, I have a bottle in my saddlebag. Would you get it and bring it over here?"

"Sure will."

When Cully brought the bottle over, Pete grabbed it and took a huge swig. He sighed. "Now I feel like I can ride."

"Just stay here for a minute. I need to go get my horse."

Samson was standing quietly where Cully had left him. He knew the horse wouldn't run off. He'd been trained well. Plus, the two of them had bonded through years of friendship. He grabbed the reins and climbed into the saddle.

"Let's go, boy. We still have a few more miles, unless Sandford slips and breaks his fool neck." He rode back to

Pete who had managed to get on his horse, whiskey bottle in hand.

He winced and smiled. "You know, I was thinking. Maybe that Comanche didn't shoot me simply because I was white. Maybe he just didn't like my singing."

Cully laughed. "Comanches aren't known for their appreciation of music."

The two started down the road, with Pete grunting constantly. Every step his horse took shot pain through his shoulder and side. He gritted his teeth and kept his hands on the reins.

Cully rode behind him. He didn't want his friend to topple from the saddle and him not know it. The tracking of Sandford was taking its toll. But that was the life of a bounty hunter.

He wasn't a storekeeper. Nor did he want to be one. He was satisfied with his life and wouldn't accept any other. At least not now. Maybe in a few years. That peaceful horse ranch he had planned began to look better and better to him. There would be a time when he would be ready to go back to Durango and take up residence as a rancher.

But not yet.

Not yet.

And not until Sandford was dead or in prison.

Chapter 13

The doctor dabbed some lotion on Pete's bloody wound and then began wrapping it with a fresh bandage. "You did a good job, Mr. Cully, in taking out the arrowhead. A lot of people could have botched that job and left Mr. Lawrence here with a bad shoulder. Probably wouldn't be able to move his arm much. But you cut that out cleanly."

"Thank you. I've done a few minor operations before," Cully said.

"You do so well, perhaps you should try the medical field. I've seen doctors who don't cut that well."

Pete chuckled. "Cully is usually putting holes into people instead of healing them.

The doctor, a man name Luther Barret, gave Cully an odd glance.

"I'm a bounty hunter and a part-time federal marshal. In my career, I have given doctors a few patients. Gave the hangman a few clients too," Cully said.

"Is that why you're here?" Barrett said.

"Yes, I think the man I'm tailing is probably now riding east of here. I'm going after him. He sold guns to some Apaches back in Colorado. I want to take him back for trial and for hanging."

"That's not going to be easy out there. It's always hot in New Mexico this time of the year, and there's no shade out there. Got some rocky flats out there and a desert. It has killed more than one person. It may save you the trouble of hanging the man."

"I don't want to leave it to chance. If the desert kills him, that's fine, but I'm taking the body back to Colorado."

"Is he worth that much?" Dr. Barret asked.

"Yes, he's got a four-figure sum on his head. I don't mind getting paid for my work."

The doctor said nothing, just pointed to the table when Pete hopped off it. "I would suggest you wait here a couple of days, Mr. Lawrence. Think you should take it easy for a day or two."

"I will. Cully is going one way, I'm going another. I'm heading off to Texas and my wedding day. The soon-to-be wife would prefer me in one piece. I want no more adventures. I'm heading for peace and quiet and good cooking."

"You've been a good partner, Pete. I appreciate it."

"Glad to help, Cully. Hope you get the guy... and get the reward too."

"Thank you. Doctor, how much do I owe you?"

"A dollar will be fine."

Cully found a bill in his pocket and handed it over. "You'll never get rich with charges that low," he said.

"I'm just trying to keep men and women alive." He smiled. "If I wanted to get rich, I would have gone into bounty hunting."

Cully laughed. He walked up to Pete and stuck out his hand. "Wish you a good life and a happy marriage, Pete. I enjoyed riding with you. You did me a big favor back there on the trail. You risked your life so I could sneak up on Sandford."

"Glad to help, my friend. Wish I could go out on the flats with you, but Betty expects me home and in one piece."

"She's marrying a good and brave man."

Pete shook Cully's hand. "Thank you. I enjoyed helping. Something I can tell Betty and eventually the grandchildren about."

"Hope you have a bushel full."

As Cully walked out, a tall, rangy man with a mustache and goatee and a badge on his vest walked up. He didn't look hostile, but there was a stern note in his voice. "You Cully or the other man?"

"I'm Cully."

"Like to talk to you. Come over to the office."

Cully nodded and followed the sheriff as he crossed the street and opened the door to his office. He was surprised that six other men had gathered there. The sheriff leaned against his desk and crossed his arms.

Cully gave a wry grin. "Sheriff, I was coming over here to tell you what happened on the trail, but I don't think the story would interest these other fellas. I'm just a bounty hunter tracking an outlaw. And he took a shot at me and my friend as we traveled to Grants. When I get through talking to you, I'll resume tracking him again."

"That's fine, Mr. Cully. I don't think I introduced myself. I'm Sheriff Lee Ransom. And I wish you luck on your tracking. But I and these gentlemen are more concerned with the attack on you and your friend. There had been rumors of Comanches in the area, but this is the first proof of it." He pointed to the other men in his office. "These gentlemen have homes and businesses in the area, so they are naturally concerned."

Cully looked at the men and nodded. "It's basically cut and dry," he started the story.

The men seemed intensely interested as Cully wove his tale of the day's events.

"Instead of fighting outlaws, I was fighting Comanches. Worked my way back to Pete, and we killed a few, then I dug the arrowhead out of him and we rode here to Grants," he finished.

"How many men were in the war party?" the sheriff asked.

"I don't know. I only saw a few. If you ride out there, you will see at least two dead on the road. I'm sure there are more, but I didn't see the main party."

A large man with dark hair, wearing what looked like a salesman's suit to Cully, spoke up. "Glad you survived, Mr. Cully. I'm Buck Tillerson. I run a clothing store here."

That explains the suit, Cully thought.

"Could those two or three warriors you saw have been the only hostiles? I'm thinking there may not have been a larger party. Just a few scouts."

"I tend to think it was only a few warriors. My mother told me never to brag on myself, but I will say I'm a good tracker and scout. A few warriors can hide in the forest, but I think I would have sensed or caught sight of a large band. I think Pete and I ran into three or four of them acting as a scouting party. Why they attacked us, I don't know. Maybe they thought three white men were easy pickin's. Also, a larger party would have reinforced the attackers. Ten or twelve Comanches are not going to run from three white men."

"He's right," Ransom said. "But we have to assume there is a larger band in the area, so we have to make plans." He reached into his pocket and brought out a telegram. "Got this from Fort Union today. A patrol of soldiers is headed this way as we speak. A contingent of fifty men. Plus there are other reinforcements on the way from another outpost. But those men will take about two days to get here. I think we should form a town militia until the Comanches are found and killed."

"I agree," Tillerson said. "We also need to send out riders to the ranches around here to tell the owners so they can prepare."

Sheriff Ransom nodded. "I'm going to form a posse to try to find the men who attacked Cully here. If they are thinking of attacking Grants, they picked the wrong town. We've got fifteen to twenty men here who fought in the Civil War. Both Southerners and Union men, but they're on the same side now. Other men stayed out of the war but know how to use a gun. Many of them have fought Indians before, so we're not going to panic. I assume all of you will volunteer?"

All six men nodded.

"I contacted Clay Bond, and he's on his way here. He's one of the best scouts in the territory, so he can handle the scouting for us. I'm also sending out telegrams to sheriffs of nearby towns, warning them to get ready for a possible attack." He looked at Cully. "Thanks for coming in, Mr. Cully. Care to join us?"

"No, thank you, sheriff. I have my own battle to fight. He's probably riding through the desert now. I wish you well, but I don't think you need me. So if you don't mind…" He tipped his hat and left the office.

He walked to the general store and bought a canteen. Traveling through a desert, he might need an extra one. He also purchased additional bullets. With the Comanche warriors and Sandford around, a few extra rounds could be useful.

Outside, he paused a moment. He pulled the tobacco pouch and cigarette papers from his shirt. He slowly spread the tobacco on one of the sheets, rolled it, licked it, and closed it. He lit the cigarette and blew out gray smoke.

He realized he was weary. He would have preferred to relax for a few days and give his body a chance to recuperate. His body ached. Back, neck, and legs let him know they wanted to rest. The aching made him realize he wanted to finish it with Sandford. He didn't want to be tracking the varmint for another week, much less months. He decided he would travel fast and try to catch Sandford before he made it across the desert. Anyone riding across a desert usually goes slow. But he wouldn't. He thought Sandford was cunning. Not necessarily all that courageous but cunning. *Sandford was a man who had courage but*, Cully thought, *used it sparingly*. He didn't look for trouble and he didn't look for fair fights. He'd much rather ambush a man than face him down in the street. So be it. He'd dealt with men like that before. They die just the same.

He walked to the saloon and bought a bottle of whiskey. Along with the bullets, the whiskey would be useful on his journey. He knew Samson was waiting for him at the livery stable. "Yes, we're heading out, Samson. One last journey."

Samson neighed and nodded his head when he saw Cully walk into the stall.

"Glad you're ready, boy. We are off again. Will be a tough trail this time, but hopefully it will be a short one. And then we go back to Colorado, back to my ranch. I think I may take a break after I get Sandford. Maybe two or three weeks. Maybe a month. Go home and get to know my sister again. Let the wounds heal." He patted the horse again. "That means you get some time off, too. Put you out in the fields and let you munch as much grass as you like and fill your stall full of hay. You'll be fat in no time."

Samson neighed again.

Chapter 14

Sweat ran down Sandford's face and neck. It had also dampened his shirt, causing the blue fabric to change to a deeper hue. His horse trudged slowly through the sand. Sandford knew Thunder was getting tired. He regretted that, but it couldn't be helped.

Thunder's legs moved slower and slower. The horse hadn't had a good feed for a couple days, although he had been fed. But the sweat poured from his skin too.

The yellow sun had no clouds to block the golden rays that turned men's skin to red, dried it out, and blistered it. Sandford looked behind him but saw only desert, rocks, and sand. A desolate sight.

As Thunder plodded through the sand, Sandford gritted his teeth and almost cried out. Sweat was not the only thing marring his shirt. Two spots of blood also soiled the fabric. And they ached with every step Thunder took. The only good thing about the wounds was they didn't slow his gun hand. He shook his head as he felt the heat rise from the desert sand and rock.

He cursed. Cully was slicing off little pieces of him every time they met. Two planned ambushes just got him wounded each time. He watched a trickle of blood flow slowly down his shirt. He needed time to rest and recuperate. The wounds wouldn't heal properly if he kept riding.

He was beginning to change his mind about running. As he looked up at the sun, New Orleans seemed a very, long way away. He'd get no rest with Cully on his tail. Maybe he'd have to have it out with the bounty hunter. One on one. The odds might be even, but that couldn't be helped. If he could find a way to shift the odds to his side...

As he looked in the distance, he could barely make out the flats but he saw them through the desert haze. The desert can do strange things to a man. It can show you things that aren't there. At least there was water soon, a large lake between the sand and the tall hill loomed where the desert became decent land again.

He choked, spit out some dust, and scratched his jaw. He'd never get away from Cully. The man would follow him to the Pearly Gates—if by some miracle he got anywhere near there—or to the gates of Hell. He would never get away from that son of a preacher man.

As sweat dripped off his jaw, he knew he'd have to end it. He would never have a moment's peace with Cully on his trail. Face him. Leave him bleeding in the sand. Or leave his own red blood in the dust. He nodded. If it continued like this, he'd leave skin and blood all over New Mexico and Texas. *Finish it.*

The lake was not that far away, maybe a mile. Two miles at most. Get to the water and let Thunder drink his fill. Then rest him. It wouldn't be long before Cully arrived. By that time, he might have a plan that would give him an edge. If not, at least there wouldn't be any surprises, like when Cully surprised him in the forest. If Cully had been an ordinary bounty hunter, he would have put a bullet in him. Or two bullets to make sure he was dead. He was lucky to be alive. Perhaps he could press his luck one more time.

He could see the lake more clearly now. The sunlight reflected off the water and shot orange spears at him. Thunder seemed to perk up, as if he smelled the water.

"I'm going to let you rest for a while, boy, when I get to the lake. Have you all ready for when Cully comes," Sandford said.

Five minutes later, he climbed down from his horse, stepped into the lake, and dunked his head beneath the water. Thunder began drinking immediately. Sandford heard the heavy slurping. As he walked out of the lake, dripping with water, Sandford smiled. He had been edgy before, nervous about the confrontation. But once the decision was made, he became calm. After all the running, the hunt would be coming to an end. He lifted his gun from his holster and checked it. Satisfied, he slipped it back into the leather.

Twenty yards from the lake, a clump of trees welcomed travelers with their large, leafy branches, offering shade from the sun. He walked over and eased down, leaning against the trunk.

"Might as well take a rest too," he said. "I'll be rested and ready when Cully comes. I imagine he'll be tired and hot from riding across the desert. Imagine he'd be mighty tired. Might slow up his draw and mess up his aim. We'll see."

He brought up his canteen and gulped some water down.

"About the best lawman I've ever seen." He snorted. Everything he had heard about the man was true. But no one mentioned the tenacity. He sighed again. His back and side hurt. But in two hours or so, his troubles with Cully would be over.

He would be rested and ready, and Cully would be dog-tired from the sun and the heat.

Probably wouldn't be a fair match.

Which, of course, was exactly how he liked it.

~****~

The best time to cross a desert is at night, Cully thought as Samson walked through the sand. It's cooler at night, and occasionally there is even a slight breeze blowing across the sand. The only problem is often the reptiles and other deadly things come out from their burrows to roam. Snakes can be a problem and not just for men. Every rider has to protect his horse. He doesn't want a rattlesnake to sink its fangs into his horse's leg. If your horse is crippled or dies in the desert, chances are you will die too, and it won't be an easy death. Cully knew he'd rather take a bullet than die of thirst. One is quick, but the other is a lingering death.

But he didn't have the option of waiting until night. He wanted to find Sandford. He didn't know the man was waiting for him at the end of the trail. He had used some of his precious water to pour over his bandanna. He used the wet cloth to wipe his face. That was another plus to traveling at night. You needed less water, so night travel increased your chances of survival.

He had traveled swiftly for the desert. Samson had cantered steadily. He was fifteen hundred pounds of muscle; none of it was fat. Samson was the finest mount he had ever had. He patted the horse.

"You're doing well, Samson. When this job is through, we'll go back home, and you will get a long rest with plenty of good food. Might take a break after kicking Sandford into a cage, or a grave. You know, Samson, I'm thinking more and more of home. Usually on a job, I think only of capturing the outlaw. Now I'm thinking more about my sister and brother-in-law and the horse ranch." He laughed. "Maybe I'm getting old."

He grimaced. The wounds sent minor jolts of pain through his back to remind him they hadn't healed yet, and the constant jarring of hooves hitting the ground didn't help the recovery. Cully just grinned and kept riding.

In the distance, he thought he saw the outlines of the lake that signified the trek across the desert was close to an end. He sighed. The sun was hot, and the heat baked the ground and rose up to hinder walkers and riders. His shirt was soaked in sweat.

After crossing the desert, Cully thought he would increase the speed of his chase. He wanted to find Sandford as soon as possible. Plus, trailing a man across rocky flats would be difficult. He couldn't let Sandford get a long way ahead of him. He would find him, eventually. He was a good tracker. But the hunt was easier when the prey didn't get too far ahead.

At first, Cully thought he was seeing things. Heat and steam rose from the desert sands and obstructed his vision. But he thought he saw a horse and rider in the distance. A dim, gray figure that wasn't moving. He shook his head and wondered if his eyes were telling the truth or muddling his brain. He reached for his gun and felt the warm metal. He spurred Samson to go faster.

The gray horse and rider hadn't moved. He frowned. If the man was Sandford, he must have given up all hope of shooting him in the back. As he rode closer, the fuzziness took on shape. The grayness wasn't a mirage. It was a real, flesh-and-blood man on a real flesh-and-blood horse. Every step Samson took made the image look more and more like Sandford. Cully smiled. The end of the trail.

The haze cleared, and Cully saw the man clearly.

It was Sandford. He had his hand on his gun.

The air was clear now. No haze. No fuzziness. Cully stopped his horse about a hundred yards from his prey.

Sandford rose up from his saddle and yelled. "Cully! You want me! You'll have to come and get me. I'm through with running."

"That's fine with me. I was getting tired of running after you."

Both men had their hand on their pistols.

"You're worse than a hound dog after a raccoon," Sandford said. "And I think you treed me. I'm gonna kill you, or I'll never have any peace in the world."

"You won't have any peace in the next one either," Cully replied. "I'll give you one chance to give up. Throw down your guns and come with me. You'll have a trial."

Sandford snorted. "Before they hang me?"

"I imagine that would be the outcome."

"There's no chance there. I'd die with my boots in the air. Easier to take you and leave the hangman behind."

"The hangman will never be behind you, Sandford. You'll die by a bullet or by a rope. You can choose. Which will it be?"

"Glad you came, Cully. I've never killed a bounty hunter, and I always wanted to. Fill your hand!"

Sandford drew his gun and rode toward him. Cully spurred Samson and drew his pistol. The two men galloped toward one another in the heat and sand. Sandford fired first but mistakenly fired when he was still out of range. The bullet plunked into the sand at Samson's feet. Firing from a galloping horse makes it difficult to aim at your target. Your hands and arms are not steady but constantly in movement. Sandford had forgotten about his wounds. The charge jarred his back and arms. His second shot went wild.

Cully fired back. He ached with every step Samson took, but he held his pistol steady and pulled the trigger.

Sandford yelled, as much with frustration as pain, when the bullet plunged into his shoulder.

The horses circled. Sandford pulled the reins and swung Thunder around to make another charge. Cully did the same with Samson.

He felt the breeze from another bullet as it shot past his ear. He aimed and fired again, but his volley went wide.

Sandford spurred his horse and charged again.

Cully started to but then held back. "No, let him come to me. Stay, Samson. Stay."

Samson did, standing as firm as a tree. As Sandford galloped toward him, Cully stretched out his arm. With Samson not moving, he took steady aim and fired twice.

Sandford jerked when the bullets left bloody holes in his chest. He wavered in the saddle while his weakened fingers dropped the gun to the sand. He gave one last death groan as he fell to the sand. After he hit the ground, he didn't move.

Cully rode over to the body and looked down at the dead man. He sighed. "My father once told the story of Cain and Able. After Able killed his brother, the Lord told him, 'Your brother's blood cries out to me from the ground.' My father said that wasn't a figure of speech. 'In the spirit world, blood has a voice,' he said, 'and the blood was crying out for justice.' So I figure the blood of people you killed also cries out for justice. Those cries have been heard. Justice has been served. Those you killed can rest in peace. And you, you murderous scum, will never have peace for all eternity."

Epilogue

Sheriff Ransom leaned against a post when he saw Cully ride in. The sheriff was surprised when he saw the bounty hunter holding the reins to a second horse tailing behind him with a body slung over the saddle. Cully nodded and turned his horse toward a hitching post in front of the sheriff's office.

"Been wondering about you," Ransom said. "Took off about five days ago. Thought maybe your man was runnin' like a jackrabbit to Texas and you had to follow him."

Cully tied Samson to the post. "Took me two days to find him. He was across the desert but decided to make a last stand." He looked back toward Sandford's body. "And it was his last stand. Then I took a day to relax by the lake there. I needed the rest. So did the horses."

Cully found the wanted poster in his pocket and showed it to Ransom. "When you check the dead man, sheriff, you'll see he's the man on this poster. I'd appreciate it if you put in a request for the reward."

Ransom took the poster. "Well, I'm sure it is, but I guess I have to check." He walked back to the second horse, grabbed the dead man by the hair, and lifted up his head, then took another quick glance at the poster. "Yep, that's him."

The sheriff's door opened, and a deputy stepped out.

"Bill, would you mind taking this guy down to the undertaker? Mr. Redstone will take care of him."

"Sure will, sheriff."

Ransom checked the pockets of the dead man and pulled out a few dollars. He snorted. "A man who sold guns to the Indians, getting people killed, and he has no money? Three dollars to pay for his funeral?"

Cully grinned. "The way of the transgressor is hard, as my father might say, and often they end up broke. My father could make a sermon out of that. But guess you can sell the horse to pay for the funeral."

The deputy grabbed the reins and started leading the horse down the street.

"Come on in, Cully," Ransom said. "I'll need you to sign a few papers. Have to fill in the names," he said, smiling. "And when Bill gets back, he needs to witness this, and then I can send it off and get the bounty wired to you."

"Thank you, sheriff."

"You did the state a favor by killing this no-good varmint. You heading back home now?"

"Sure am. Oh, know anything more about the renegade Comanches? Do I need to be on the lookout when I ride back?"

Ransom shook his head. "Nope. Three days after you left, the town militia, and the cavalry battled them about eight miles west of here. Killed about three dozen, and the rest scattered. You should have a peaceful trip back home."

"Good to hear." Cully sighed

"Will you be off hunting again soon?"

Cully shook his head. "No, not for a while. I'm going to take time to let the wounds heal, do a little fishing, and visit with my sister for a long time. As my father might say, there is a time for everything, a time to be born and a time to die, a time to kill and a time to heal, a time for war and a time for peace. This is a time for peace and healing. A time to go home and be with family."

Ransom nodded. "I understand."

The End

Could I get you to consider leaving a review on Amazon? It would be appreciated.

More westerns are in the works.

Made in the USA
Monee, IL
12 November 2025